The Tough Guys

Mickey
Spillane

Ⓢ

A SIGNET BOOK from
NEW AMERICAN LIBRARY
TIMES MIRROR

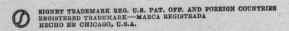

SIGNET TRADEMARK REG. U.S. PAT. OFF. AND FOREIGN COUNTRIES
REGISTERED TRADEMARK——MARCA REGISTRADA
HECHO EN CHICAGO, U.S.A.

SIGNET, SIGNET CLASSICS, SIGNETTE, MENTOR AND PLUME BOOKS
are published by The New American Library, Inc.,
1301 Avenue of the Americas, New York, New York 10019

FIRST PRINTING, DECEMBER, 1969

PRINTED IN THE UNITED STATES OF AMERICA

Contents

"KICK IT OR KILL!"

An old switcher engine pulled the two-car train from the junction at Richfield over the 12-mile spur into Lake Rappaho. At the right time the ride could have been fun because the cars were leftovers from another era, but now it was a damn nuisance. Coal dust had powdered everything, settling into the mohair seats like sand and hanging in the air so you could taste it. Summer was two months gone and the mountains and valleys outside were funneling down cold Canadian air. There was no heat in the car.

Ordinarily, I wouldn't have minded, but now the chill made my whole side ache again under the bandage and I was calling myself an idiot for listening to that doctor and his wild ideas about me having to take a complete rest. I could have holed up just as well in New York, but instead I fell for the fresh air routine and took his advice about this place.

Lake Rappaho was the end of the line. A single limp

sack of mail and a half dozen packages came off the baggage car as I stepped down from the last one.

On the other side of the platform, a black '58 Chevy with a hand painted *TAXI* on its door stood empty. I saw the driver, all right. He and a wizened old stationmaster were in the office peering at me like I was a stray moose in church. But that's mountain country for you. When you're out of season and not expected, everybody goes into a G.I. hemorrhage.

I waved my thumb at the taxi, picked up my old B-4 bag and the mailing tube I kept my split bamboo rod in, walked across the station to the car, threw my gear in the back seat, then got in front for the drive into Pinewood. It was another five minutes before the driver came out.

He opened the door on the other side. "Afternoon. You going to Pinewood?"

"Anyplace else to go?"

He shook his head. "Not for fifty miles, I guess."

"Then let's go there."

He slid under the wheel and kicked the motor over. In backing around the corner of the station he made a pretense of seeing my duffel in the back. "You going fishing?"

"That's the general idea."

"No fishing now, you know. Wrong season."

"It's still open, isn't it?"

He nodded. "For the rest of the month. But there's no fish."

"Shut up," I said.

It was a four-mile trip into the fading sun to Pinewood and he didn't say anything again, but every foot of the way his hands were white around the wheel.

Pinewood had a permanent population of 2,500. It lay where the valley widened on one end of Lake Rappaho, a mile and a half long and four blocks wide. The summer cabins and homes on the outskirts were long closed and what activity there was centered around the main crossroads.

The Pines Hotel stood on the corner, a three-story white frame building whose second-story porch overhung the entire width of the sidewalk.

I paid the cabby, grabbed my luggage and went inside.

The two big guys bordering the door waited until I had crossed the lobby and was at the desk. Then they came up and watched while I signed the register. The heavy one took my card from the clip and looked at it.

"Mister Kelly Smith, New York City," he said. "That's a big place for a whole address."

"Sure is." The clerk edged up from his desk with a small, fixed smile divided between the other two and me.

"I'll be here two weeks," I told him. "I want a room upstairs away from the sun and take it out in advance." I pushed a hundred dollar bill across the desk and waited.

"Like if somebody wanted to find you in New York . . ." the big guy started to say.

I snatched the card from his fingers. "Then you look in the phone book. I'm listed," I said. I was feeling the old edge come back.

"Smith is a common name . . ."

"I'm the only Kelly Smith."

He tried to stare me down, but I wasn't playing any games. So instead he reached out and picked up my C note and looked at it carefully. "Haven't seen one of these in a long time."

I took that away from him too. "The way you're going you'll never see one," I said.

The clerk smiled, his eyes frightened, took the bill, and gave me $16 back. He handed me a room key. "Two-nineteen, on the corner."

The big guy touched me on the shoulder. "You're pretty fresh."

I grinned at him. "And you're a lousy cop. Now just get off my back or start conducting a decent investigation. If it'll make you happy, I'll be glad to drop by your office, give you a full B.G., let you take my prints, and play Dragnet all you want. But first I want to get cleaned up and get something to eat."

He suddenly developed a nervous mouth. "Supposing you do that. You do just that, huh?"

"Yeah," I said. "Later maybe," and watched him go out.

When the door closed the clerk said. "That was Captain Cox and his sergeant, Hal Vance."

"They always pull that act on tourists?"

"Well, no . . . no, of course not."

"How many are in the department here."

"The police? Oh . . . six, I think."

"That's two too many. They pull that stunt on me again while I'm here and I'll burn somebody's tail for them."

Behind me, a voice with a cold, throaty quality said, "I don't know whether I want you here or not."

I glanced at the clerk. "Nice place you run here. Who is she?"

"The owner." He nodded to a hand-carved plaque on his desk. It read, Miss Dari Dahl, Prop.

She was a big one, all right, full breasted and lovely with loose sun-bleached hair touching wide shoulders and smooth, tanned skin.

"You haven't any choice, honey. I got a receipt for two weeks. Now smile. A lovely mouse like you ought to be smiling all the time."

She smiled. Very prettily. Her mouth was lush like I knew it would be and she hip-tilted toward me deliberately. Only her eyes weren't smiling. She said, "Drop dead, you creep," and brushed by me.

There was something familiar about her name. The clerk gave me the answer. "It was her sister who killed herself in New York last year. Flori Dahl. She went out a window of the New Century Building."

I remembered it then. It made headlines when she landed on a parked U.N. car and almost killed a European delegate about to drive off with a notorious call girl. The tabloids spilled the bit before the hush needles went in.

"Tough," I said, "only she oughtn't to let it bug her like that."

I had supper in White's restaurant. I had a table in the corner where I could see the locals filter in to the bar up front. The few who ate were older couples and when they were done I was alone. But everybody knew where I was. They looked at me often enough. Not direct, friendly glances, but scared things that were touched with some hidden anger.

My waitress came over with a bill. I said softly, "Sugar . . . what the hell's the matter with this town?"

She was scared, too. "Sir?" was all she could manage.

I walked up to the bar.

At 8 o'clock, Captain Cox and Sergeant Vance came in and tried to make like they weren't watching me. Fifteen minutes later, Dari Dahl came in. When she finally saw me her eyes became veiled with contempt, then she turned away and that was that.

I was ready to go when the door opened again. You could feel the freeze. Talk suddenly quieted down. The two guys in tweedy coats closed the door behind them and walked up to the bar with studied casualness. Their clothes were just the right kind, but on the wrong people because they weren't Madison Avenuers at all. One was Nat Paley and the bigger guy you called Lennie Weaver when you wanted to stay friends, but, if you had a yen for dying quick, you gave him the Pigface tab Margie Provetsky hung on him years ago.

I felt that crazy feeling come all over me and I wanted to grin, but for now I kept it in. I pushed my stool back and that's as far as I got. The little guy who stormed in was no more than 20, but he had an empty milk bottle in one hand and he mouthed a string of curses as he came at Paley and Weaver.

Trouble was, he talked too much. He tried to spill it out before he cut loose. Lenny laced him with a sudden backhand as Nat grabbed him, took the bottle away, and slammed him to the floor.

He wasn't hurt, but he was too emotionally gone to do anything more than cry. His face was contorted with hate.

Lenny grunted and picked up his drink. "You crazy, kid?"

"You dirty bastard!" The words were softly muffled. "You talked her into working for him."

"Get outa here, kid."

"She didn't have to work up there. She had a job. You showed her all that money, didn't you? That's why she worked. She always talked about having that kind of money. You bastards! You dirty bastards!"

When Nat kicked him, the blood splashed all over his shoes and the kid just lay there. He twitched, vomited, and started to choke. The only one who moved was Dari.

She managed to get him face down and held him like that until he moaned softly and opened his eyes.

She glanced up with those wild eyes of hers and said, "Sonny was right. You're dirty bastards."

"Would you like a kick in the face too, lady?" Lennie asked her.

For a second it was real quiet, then I said, "Try it, Pig-face."

He spun around and my shoe ripped his sex machine apart and while he was in the middle of a soundless scream I grabbed Nat's hair and slammed his face against the bar. He yelled, swung at me, and one hand tore into the bandage over my ribs and I felt the punk draining right out of me. But that was his last chance. I almost brained him the next time and let him fall in a heap on the floor with his buddy.

I faked a grin at Dari, walked past the two cops at the table, and said so everybody could hear me, "Nice clean town you got here, friend," and went outside to get sick.

The window was open and I could see my breath in the air, but just the same I was soaked with sweat. When the knock came on the door I automatically said to come on in, not caring who it was. My side was one gigantic ball of fire and it was going to be another hour before the pills I had taken helped.

There was no sympathy in her voice. The disdain was still there, only now it was touched by curiosity. She stood there, her stomach flat under her dress, her breasts swelling out, and I remembered pictures of the Amazons and thought that she would have made a good one. Especially naked.

"Sonny asked me to thank you."

Trying to make my voice sound real wasn't easy. "No trouble."

"Do you . . . know what you're doing?"

She paused.

"What do you want in Pinewood?"

"A vacation, kitten. Two weeks. I have to do it. Now, will you do me a favor?" I closed my eyes. The fire in my side was building up again.

"Yes?"

"In my flight bag over there . . . in the side pocket is a bottle of capsules. Please . . ."

I heard the zipper run back, then the sharp intake of her breath. The gun she found in the wrong side pocket suddenly fell to the floor with a thump and then she was standing over me again. She had the bottle in her hand.

"You're a damned drug addict, aren't you? That's the way they get without their dosage. They get sick, they sweat, they shake." She poured the caps back in the bottle and capped it. "Your act in the restaurant stunk. Now act this one out." With a quick flip of her wrist she threw the bottle out the window and I heard it smash in the street.

"You filth," she said and walked out.

It was three in the afternoon when I woke up. I lay there panting and, when the sudden sickness in my stomach subsided, I got to my feet and undressed. Outside, a steady light rain tapped against the windows.

A hot shower was like a rebirth.

The .45 was still on the floor where Dari Dahl had let it drop and I hooked it with my foot, picked it up, and zippered it inside my leather shaving kit.

Every time I thought of that crazy broad throwing that bottle out the window I felt like laying her out. That wasn't getting those capsules back, though. I had maybe another two hours to go and I was going to need them bad, bad, bad. I stuffed 50 bucks in my pocket and went downstairs.

Outside my window, I found the remains of the bottle. The capsules inside had long since dissolved and been washed away by the rain.

I shrugged it off, found the drugstore and passed my spare prescription over to the clerk. He glanced at it, looked at me sharply, and said, "This will take an hour."

"Yeah, I know. I'll be back."

I headed for the restaurant. Although lights were on in store fronts and the corner traffic blinker winked steadily, there wasn't a car or a person on the street. It was like a ghost town.

The restaurant was empty. The waitress recognized me with a peculiar smile, took my order, and half-ran to the kitchen. The bartender walked across the room to me.

He was a graying man in his late 40s, a little too thin with deep tired eyes. "Look, mister," he said, "I don't want trouble in here."

I leaned back in my chair. "You know who those jokers were?"

He nodded. "We'll handle things our own way."

"Then start by keeping out of my hair, friend," I told him. "I don't know how or why those punks are here, but they're the kind of trouble people like you just don't handle at all, so be grateful for the little things, understand?"

He didn't understand at all and his face showed it. He glanced outside toward the distant slope of the mountain. "You aren't . . . on the hill?"

"Mac, I don't know what the hell you're talking about. I think you people are nuts, that's all. I pull those punks off the kid's back last night while you, the cops, and everybody else just watch and *I* catch the hard time. I don't get it."

The door slammed open and Sergeant Vance came in. He came sidling over and tossed a sheet of paper down on the table. It was my prescription.

"This calls for narcotics, mister. You better come up with a damn good explanation."

Real slowly I stood up. Vance was a big guy, but he wasn't looking down on me at all. Not at all. His face was all mean but scared too like the rest and his hand jumped to the butt of his service revolver.

I said, "Okay, you clown, I'll give you one explanation and if you ask again I'll shove that gun of yours up your pipe. That's a legitimate prescription you got there and, if you do any checking, you check the doctor who issued it first. Then, if it's bad, you come back to me. Meanwhile, you have a certain procedure to take that's down in black and white in the statute books. Now you take that prescription back and see that it gets filled or you'll be chewing on a warrant for your own arrest."

He got it, all right. For a minute, I thought I was going to have to take the rod away from him, but the message got through in time. He went out as fast as he came in.

What a hell of a vacation this was. Brother!

Willie Elkins, who owned a garage, was willing to

rent me his pickup truck for 15 bucks a week. It was a dilapidated thing, but all I needed. He told me how to find old Mort Steiger, who rented boats. The old guy let me have my pick, then shook his head at me and grinned through his broken plate. "You ain't no fisherman, are you?"

"Nope," I shook back. "I try once in a while, but I'm no fisherman."

He paused, watching me warily. "You on the hill?"

"What is this 'hill' business? Who's up on what hill?"

He waited a moment, sucking on his lips. "You kiddin'? No, guess you ain't." He pointed a gnarled finger over my shoulder. "Big place up there just around that ridge. Can't see it from here, but she has a private road that comes right down to the lake, all fenced in. Whole place like that. You can't get in or out unless they let you."

"Who lets you?"

"City people. That's Mister Simpson's place. Big manufacturer of something or other. Never met him myself. He likes it private."

I let out a grunt. "He sure does. He has a real goon squad working for him. I met a couple last night. They needed straightening out."

This time his grin got broader and he chuckled. "So you're the one. Willie told me about that. Could be you'll make trouble for yourself, if you don't watch out."

"It won't come from two-bit punks, pop. Trouble is, if Simpson's such a big one, what's he doing with guys like that on his place?"

"Maybe I could tell you."

I waited.

"This Simpson feller was a big one long time ago. Bootlegging or something, then he went straight. He had all this money so he went into business. Few times a year he comes up here, does some business, and leaves."

"Everybody in town is scared, pop. That's not good business."

His eyes seemed to scratch the ground. "Ain't the business he does."

"What then?"

"The girls. He sends down to Pinewood for girls."

"The place looks big enough to support a few hookers."

"Mister, you just don't know country towns. Comes end of summer and *those* girls pack up and leave. It's the others he gets."

"Listen, a guy that big wouldn't try . . ."

He interrupted with a wave of his hand. "You got me wrong. He . . . employs them."

"Well, what's wrong with that?"

"They go up there, all right, but they don't come back . . . well, the same . . . Rita Moffet and the oldest Spencer girl moved over to Sunbar. Bob Rayburn's only girl, she never would speak to anybody and last year they had to send her to the State Hospital. She still won't speak to anybody at all. Flori Dahl and Ruth Gleason went off to New York. Flori died there and nobody has heard from Ruth in months."

"Nice picture."

"Others, too. That's not all. Some are still here and every time Simpson and the bunch comes in they go up there to work. Like they enjoy it. He pays them plenty, oh, you can bet that. What stuff they buy, and all from New York."

"Any complaints?"

The old man frowned. "That's the funny part. None of 'em say nothing."

I stood up and stretched. "You know what I think? This Simpson guy pays them mighty generously and for the first time they get a look at how the other half lives and want to give it a try. So they leave town. It's an old story. The others won't leave, but let the gravy come to them. How about that?"

"He got funny people working for him. They bring trouble to town, mister."

"Okay, so he hires hoods. I know reputable businessmen who have done the same."

Steiger thought it over. "Maybe, but did you ever see such a scared town in your life, mister?"

The drizzle had stopped. I zippered up my jacket and shoved my hat on. Mort Steiger watched me carefully.

Finally he said, "You're a funny one, too, mister."

"Oh?"

"You got a real mean look. You're big and you look mean. You tell me something true?"

I opened the door of the pickup and said over my shoulder, "Sure I'll tell you true, pop."

"You ever kill anybody?"

I slammed the door shut and looked at him. He was completely serious.

Finally I nodded. "Yes. Six people."

"I don't mean in the war, son."

"I wasn't talking about the war."

"How'd you do it?"

"I shot them," I said and let the clutch out.

The druggist had my prescription ready and handed it over without a word. I knew he had checked on the doctor who issued it and had another check going through different channels. I ordered a Coke, took two of the capsules, and pocketed the rest.

A fresh rain slick was showing on the street and the weather forecast was that it would continue for a few days. So I'd fish in the rain. I'd take a six-pack of Blue Ribbon and a couple sandwiches along and anchor in the middle of the lake under an umbrella.

I went outside, flipped a mental coin to see where I'd eat. The coffee shop in the hotel won and I hopped in the truck. At the corner the blinker was red on my side and I rolled to a stop. As I did, a new black Caddy with Kings County (New York) plates made the turn and I had a fast look at the driver.

His name was Benny Quick, he had done two turns in Sing Sing on felony counts and was supposedly running a dry-cleaning place in Miami. There was somebody beside him and somebody in the back, but I couldn't make them out.

I made a U turn, passed the sedan, turned right two blocks farther on, and let the Caddy pass behind me. That's all I needed to pick up the license number. A friend back in New York would do the rest.

I couldn't figure what Benny Quick was doing up this way, but I made a living being nosy and I had been too long at it to let a vacation take me out of the habit.

Back at the Pines Hotel, I shared the coffee shop with

a half dozen teen-agers sipping coffee and feeding the juke box. None of them paid any attention to me. The waitress snapped the menu down in front of me.

When I looked up I said, "You ought to smile more, Miss Dahl."

"Not for you, Mr. Smith."

"Call me Kelly."

She ignored me completely and waited. I told her what I wanted, and while I waited scanned a newspaper. The headlines were still all about football.

Dari Dahl came back, fired my cheeseburgers at me, and put the coffee down so hard it spilled. I said, "Go back and get me another cup."

"What?"

"Damn it, you heard me. I've had about all the crap from you I can take. You be as sore as you please, but, baby, treat me like a customer or for kicks I'll throw these dishes through your front window. This town is giving me the business and from now on the business stops. Now shake your butt and get me another coffee and do it right."

The next time the coffee came slow and easy. I said, "Sit down."

She paused. "Mr. Smith . . ."

When I looked up and she saw my face, she grew chalky and pulled out a chair.

Dari Dahl was a magnificent woman, even scared. The tight nylon uniform outlined the daring cut of her underthings. The word bra was disputable for all that it was, and below it, far below, was a bikini-like thing beautifully discernible.

"I heard about your sister," I said.

"Let's not discuss it."

"Dari baby, it won't be too hard to find out someplace else. I remember the rough details. Any old newspaper account could fill me in. Anybody around town ought to be glad to talk about the bit."

The hardness came back again, her mouth pulling tight at the corners. "You should be able to understand it. My sister was a drug addict, when she could no longer supply her need, she killed herself. Eventually, you'll do the same."

"I will?"

"Your supposed legitimate source of supply through our druggist won't last very long. My sister used stolen and forged prescriptions, too, for a while. It was when they ran out that she killed herself." She stopped, her eyes glinting. "Tell me, Mr. Smith, are you here now because there are no other pharmacists who will honor your prescriptions? Is that it?"

Slowly, I finished my coffee. "You really are bugged, kid. You really are."

She walked away, tall, cool, a lovely, curvy animal, as beautiful as any woman ever was, but going completely to waste.

I left a buck and a half by my plate, went upstairs where I showered and changed into a city suit. I decided to try the air again. There should be a movie or a decent bar someplace.

I reached for the phone, but remembered the clerk downstairs and hung up. In the lobby, I called from a house phone where I could watch the desk, gave a New York number, and waited.

When my number answered, I said, "Artie?"

"Yeah, hi ya, Kelly, how's it going?"

For a full five minutes we made idle conversation about nothing, throwing in enough dirty words so any prudish operator bugging in would knock it off in disgust. Then I said, "Run a number through for me, kid, then get me all the information on its owner. Next, find out what you can about Benny Quick. He's supposed to be in Miami." I fed him the license number, talked a little more about nothing, and hung up.

Outside, the rain had started again, harder this time. I looked each way, saw a couple of recognizable lights, grinned, and walked toward them.

Like a whore's is red, police lights have to be green, old-fashioned, and fly-specked. You knew from the sight of them what it's going to smell like inside. There's a man smell of wet wool, cigars, and sweat. There's a smell of wood, oiled-down dust; of stale coffee, and musty things long stored. On top of that, there's another smell a little more quiet, one of fear and shame that comes from the other people who aren't cops and who go down forever in the desk book.

I walked in and let Sergeant Vance stare at me like a snake and then said, "Where's your captain?"

"What do you want him for?"

The pair of young beat cops who had been standing in the corner moved in on the balls of their feet. They were all set to take me when the office door opened and Cox said, "Knock it off, Woody." He ran his eyes up and down me. "What do you want?"

I grinned at him, but it wasn't friendly at all. "You wanted my prints, remember? You said to stop by."

He flushed, then his jaw went hard. He came out of the doorway and faced me from three feet away. "You're a rough character, buddy. You think we don't know what to do with rough guys?"

And I gave it to him all the way. I said, "No, I don't think you know what to do with rough guys, Captain. I think you're all yak and nothing else."

Across his forehead, a small pulse beat steadily. But he held it in better than I thought he could. His voice was hard but restrained when he told the beat cop behind me, "Take his prints, Woody."

I gave him my name and address and stopped right there. If he wanted anything on me he could get it only after he booked me. I grinned at everybody again, left a bunch of stinking mad cops behind me, and went out into the fresh air.

It was 9 o'clock, too late for a show but not for a bar. I found one called JIMMIE'S with Jimmie himself at the bar and ordered a beer. Jimmie was a nice old guy and gassed with me.

When I finally got around to the Simpson place, he made a wry face and said, "Nobody ever saw the guy I know of. Not down here in town."

"How about the girls?"

He nodded. "You don't get much out of them. Simpson turns out to be either big or little, skinny or fat and you get the point. They don't talk it up any."

"So they don't talk about their boss. They get paid plenty, I hear."

"Hell, yes. Bonnie Ann and Grace Shaefer both sport

minks and throw plenty of bucks around. Every once in a while I see Helen Allen in a new car. She comes through about once a month to see her folks. Used to be a nice kid. All of them were."

"Making money changed that?"

Jimmie shook his head, squinting. "No, but used to be they were plain hustlers and not high on anybody's list."

I asked, "You mean that's their job up there?"

His shrug was noncommittal. "They won't say. Some of them do secretarial work, answering phones and all that, because the switchboard operators here have talked to them often enough."

"If they're that interested, why doesn't somebody just ring Simpson's bell and ask?"

Jimmie gave a short laugh. "Besides the brush-off at the gate, who wants to spoil a good thing? Before that bunch leaves there'll be a bunch of money in this town, and off season you don't kick out found loot. Then there's another angle. That boy's a big taxpayer. He's got connections where they count, as some busybodies found out. A few local do-gooders tried some snooping and wound up holding their behinds. Nobody goes to the cops, though I can't see them doing much about it. Cox is like a cat who's afraid of a mouse yet getting hungry enough so he knows he has to eat one or die. I think he figures if he eats one it'll be poisoned and he'll die, too."

He opened me another bottle and moved on down the bar to take care of a new customer. It was the nervous taxi driver who tried to steer me away from Pinewood in the first place. I was beginning to wish I had let him talk me into it.

He ordered a beer, too, said something about the weather, then confidentially told Jimmie, "Saw somebody tonight. Didn't recognize her at first, but it was Ruth Gleason."

I poured my glass full, making like I was concentrating on it. Ruth Gleason was the girl Mort Steiger told me ran off to New York the same time Flori Dahl did.

"You sure?" Jimmie asked him.

"Oughta know her, I guess. She's changed though. She's got on fancy clothes and all that, but her face is sure old looking. Wouldn't look at me. She kind of turned away when she saw me."

"Well what's she doing back here?"

"Who knows? She got in that blue ranchwagon from the hill place and drove off." He waved off another beer and went out.

Jimmie came back wiping his hands on his apron.

Bluntly, I said, "Mort told me about the Gleason kid, too."

He didn't question my tone. "Nice girl. She was up there a whole month. Hardly ever came down and when she did she wouldn't speak to anybody. Flori and she went in at the same time. Flori used to come to town occasionally and the way she changed was hard to believe."

"How?"

He waved his hands expressively. "Like you can't pin it down. Just changed. They wouldn't look at you or hardly speak. It was real queer."

"Didn't any of those kids have parents?"

"Flori's old man was dying and they had no mother. I think Flori took the job up there to help get her old man into the Humboldt Hospital. They got him there, but he died soon after. Cancer."

"That's only one," I pointed out.

"Ah, who can tell kids anyhow? They do what they please anyway. Sure, some of them had folks, but there's big money up there."

He popped the top from another bottle and passed it over. "On the house." He took a short one himself and we gave a silent toast and threw them down.

Then he said, "Better not do too much talking around town. This is a spooky place."

I grinned, paid off my tab, and waved him good night.

For a few minutes I stood under the awning watching the rain, then started back toward the center of town. I had crossed the street and almost reached the corner when the big Imperial came from my left, turned left, and stopped half a block up ahead of me. Unconsciously, I stepped into the darker shadows and walked faster.

Someone stepped out of the car, turned and pulled at another. They stood there together a moment and then I heard the unmistakable spasm of a sob.

I ran then, holding one hand tight against my ribs to muffle the fire that had started there. I was too late. They heard my feet pounding and the one by the car turned sharply, ducked inside, and slammed the door. The car pulled away silently and slowly as if nothing had happened.

But they left a beautiful young girl behind them. She was sobbing hysterically and started to collapse as I reached her.

She was a lovely brunette wrapped tightly in a white trenchcoat, her hair spilling wetly over her shoulders. She tried to shove me away while she hung on desperately to an oversize handbag and keep saying over and over, "No . . . please, no!"

I said, "Easy, kid," and pulled her to the porch steps of the nearest house. When I got her seated I tried to take her hand. She stopped sobbing then, jerked her hand, and held her pocketbook on the opposite side.

For a second the hysteria passed and she said, "Get out of here. Let me alone!"

"Relax, I'm . . ."

"There's nothing the matter with me," she nearly shouted. "Get out of here. *Let me alone!*"

She clenched her teeth on the last word with a crazy grimace and tried to stand up. But I was sitting on one edge of her coat and when she did the thing yanked open and half-pulled off her shoulder.

She was naked from the waist up and I didn't need any light to see the welts and stripes across her body and the small bleeding spots where something with a sharp tip had dug in.

I stood up, pulled the trench coat closed. When she realized I had seen her, she closed her eyes, let out a soft mewing sound, and let herself fold up in my arms. I put her down on the steps again and as I did, her pocketbook fell open. There was a sheaf of brand new bills inside, held by a bank wrapper. On it was printed the number *1,000*.

Suddenly the porch light snapped on, the door opened, and a man stood there clutching his bathrobe at his middle. His wife peered over his shoulder, her face worried.

"You," he called out. "What are you doing there?" His voice didn't have too much snap to it.

I motioned to the girl. "There's a sick woman here. Look, call a doctor for me and hurry it, will you?"

"A doctor? What's . . ."

"Never mind what's the matter. You call. And turn out that light."

They were glad to get back inside. The porch light went out and inside one turned on. I propped the kid up, put her bag under her arm, and walked away from the house.

I didn't get very far. The car hissed up behind me and a voice said, "It's him again. The one who jumped Lennie and me in the restaurant."

There wasn't any sense running. A dozen fast steps would tear my side anyway. I just stood there and because I did the action that was all set to explode went sour. Nat Paley and the new guy who hopped out and came at me from different sides slowed, not able to figure me out.

Nat's hand came out of his pocket with a gun. The gun came up and Nat's face said it was the right time and the right place. Except somebody else thought differently and a strangely cold voice from inside the car said, "No noise."

They moved before I could yell. The other guy came in fast from the side, but I ducked in time to get the load in his fist off the top of my head. I kicked out, jabbed at his eyes, and made the touch. He couldn't yell with the sudden pain, ducked into my right and his face seemed to come apart under my knuckles.

And that was the end of it. Nat got me just right, one stunning blow behind the ear and, as I sank to my knees, went over me expertly with a clubbed gun and ruthless feet. As one terrible kick exploded into my side, I thought I screamed and knew with absolute certainty that Nat had one more blow to deliver. It would come with bone-crushing force in that deadly spot at the base of the brain. I knew it was coming and I hoped it would, anything that would erase the awful thing that was happening to me inside.

It came all right, but a sudden convulsion that wracked

my side made it miss and my shoulder took it all. Nat didn't realize that, though. A tiny part of my mind that could still discern things heard him laugh and drag the other guy into the car.

In the middle of a wild dream of sound and light I coughed, tried to turn my head away from the jarring, acrid fumes of ammonia, and then swam back into a consciousness I didn't want.

Somebody had carried me to the steps and a face peered anxiously into mine. The old guy watching me said, "It's all right. I'm Doctor McKeever."

"The girl . . ." I started.

"She's all right. She's inside. We'd better get you in there, too."

"I'm fine."

"What happened? Was there an accident?"

I shook my head, clearing it. "No . . . not actually."

When I moved my arm my shoulder muscles screamed. At least nothing was broken. I'd taken some bad ones before, but this took the cake. Under the bandages I could feel the warmth of blood and knew what was happening.

I said, "You saw the girl?"

"Yes."

"You got an idea of what happened?"

He chewed his lips a moment and nodded. "I know."

"You've seen it before, haven't you?"

At first he wasn't going to say anything, then he looked at me again. His voice had an edge to it. "Yes."

"Then you do like you did before, doc. You keep this under your hat, too. Let it get out and that kid is ruined here in town. She can be ruined no matter where she goes and it isn't worth a public announcement."

"Somebody has got to stop it," he said.

I said, "It'll be stopped, doc. It'll be stopped."

A small frown furrowed his forehead. His smile was crooked. "Toxin-anti-toxin," he said.

"What?"

"Poison against poison."

I nodded, spit, and said, "You go take care of that kid, then ride me back to the hotel."

When he had left I got sick again. I had to get those

capsules I had left in my room. In just a few minutes now it was going to be worse than it ever had been and I'd be a raving maniac without a big jolt from the small bottle.

I couldn't tell how long he had been gone, but finally he came out leading the girl. A car pulled around from the side and the doctor bundled her into it, telling the driver to take her to his office and deliver her to his wife.

As soon as the car left, he had me on my feet, got me in his Ford, and started up. At the hotel he got out, opened my door, and took the arm on my good side to lead me in.

Dari Dahl was behind the desk, in white nylon no longer. She was wearing a black sweater and skirt combination that dramatized every curve of her body and making the yellow of her hair look like a pool of light.

The brief flicker of concern that hit her face turned to a peculiar look of satisfaction. She came around the desk, tiny lines playing at the corner of her mouth and said, "Trouble?"

"What else. Now get my key, please."

She smiled, went back, picked the key out, and came over and handed it to me. "Are you hurting, Mr. Smith?"

Both of us shot her funny looks.

"Is it true that when a narcotic addict tries to lay off he fights it until he's almost tortured to death before he takes a dose?"

McKeever said, "What are you talking about, Dari?"

"Ask him." She smiled too sweetly.

"She's bugged, doc, let's go."

We walked to the stairs, started up them, when Dari called, "Mr. Smith . . ."

I stopped, knowing somehow what was coming.

"Quite accidentally I dropped a bottle of capsules while cleaning your room. They fell down the toilet." She stopped, letting it sink in, then added, "And so did several prescriptions that were with the bottle. I hope you don't mind too much."

She could see the sweat that beaded my face and laughed. I could hear it all the way up the steps.

I flopped on the bed and it was then, when my coat came open, that McKeever saw the blood. He opened my shirt, saw the red seeping through the bandages, took one look at the color of my face, and rushed out.

Lying there, my ribs wouldn't flex to my breathing and the air seemed to whistle in my throat. It was like being branded; only the iron never left.

The door opened and I thought it was McKeever back, then I smelled the fragrance of her across the room. My eyes slitted open. She wasn't wearing that funny smile she had before.

"What the hell do you want?" I managed to get out.

"Doctor McKeever told me . . ." she paused and moistened her lips, "about Gloria Evans. You tried to help her."

"So what?" I said nastily.

"You tried to help Sonny Holmes the other night, too."

"Sure, I'm everybody's buddy."

I closed my eyes, trying to control my breathing. She said softly, a still determined tone in her voice, "About the other thing . . . drugs. I'm not sorry about that at all."

McKeever came in then, panting from the run up the stairs. He uncovered me, got his fingers under the bandage and worked it off. He said, "A doctor took care of you, didn't he?"

All I could do was nod.

I smelled the flower smell of her as she came closer and heard the sharp intake of her breath as she saw me. "What . . . happened?"

"This man has been shot. He's recuperating from an operation." I heard Dr. McKeever open the bag and the clink of bottles. "Didn't you have anything to take periodically to kill the pain?"

I nodded again, my face a pool of sweat. I felt the needle go in my arm and knew it would be all right soon. I said through teeth held so tight they felt like they'd snap off, "Capsules. Morphine sulphate."

"Oh, no!" Her voice sounded stunned.

McKeever said, "What?"

"I thought he was a drug addict. I destroyed them."

The doctor said nothing.

Slowly the pain was lifting like a fog. Another second and I'd sleep.

Tonelessly, Dari said, "How he must hate me!"

Then I was past answering her.

It stopped raining on Wednesday. For two days I had lain there listening to my bedside radio. The hourly news broadcasts gave the latest U.N. machinations, then into the Cuban affair. Now the finger was pointing at Cuba as being the new jumping off place for narcotic shipments to the States. Under suspected Soviet sponsorship, the stuff came in easily and cheaply from China—a cleverly different kind of time bomb a country can use to soften an enemy.

But two days were enough. I found my clothes, shaved, dressed, and tried to work the stiffness out of my muscles. Even then, the stairs almost got me. I took it easy going down, trying to look more unconcerned than I felt.

McKeever wasn't glad to see me. He told me I had no business being up yet and told me to sit down while he checked the bandage. When he finished he said, "I never asked about that gunshot wound."

"Go on."

"I assume it has been reported."

"You assume right."

"However, I'm going to report it again."

"Be my guest, doc. To save time I suggest you get the doctor's name from the prescription I had filled here."

"I will." He got up and reached for the phone.

The druggist gave him the doctor's name, then he called New York. When the phone stopped cackling, McKeever nodded, "It was reported, all right. Those prescriptions were good. Then you really are here on . . . a vacation."

"Nobody seems to believe it."

"You've been causing talk since you came."

"What about the girl?" I said. "Gloria Evans."

He slumped back in his chair. "She's all right. I have her at my wife's sister's place."

"She talk?"

The doctor shook his head. "No, they never talk." He took a deep breath, tapped his fingers against the desk and said, "She was badly beaten, but there was a marked peculiarity about it. She was *carefully* beaten. Two instruments were used. One appears to be a long, thin belt; the other a fine braided whip-like thing with a small metal tip."

I leaned forward. "Punishment?"

McKeever shook his head. "No. The instruments used were too light. The application had too deliberate a pattern to it."

"There were others like that?"

"I took care of two of them. It wasn't very pretty, but they wouldn't talk. What happened to them would never leave permanent scars . . . but there are other ways of scarring people."

"One thing more, doc. Were they under any narcotic influence at all?"

McKeever sighed deeply. "Yes. The Evans girl had two syringe marks in her forearm. The others had them too, but I didn't consider them for what they were then."

I stood up. "Picture coming through, doc?"

He looked like he didn't want to believe it. "It doesn't seem reasonable."

"It never does," I told him.

I stopped at the hotel and took the .45 from my shaving kit. I checked the load, jacked one in the chamber and let the hammer down easy, then shoved it under my belt on my good side. I dropped a handful of shells in my coat pocket just in case. In the bathroom I washed down two of my capsules, locked my door, and went downstairs.

The clerk waved me over. "New York call for you, Mr. Smith. Want me to get the number back? It was paid."

I told him to go ahead. It was Artie on the other end and after helloing me he said, "I have your items for you, Kelly."

"Go ahead."

"One, the car belongs to Don Casales. He's a moderate-sized hood from the L.A. area and clean. Casales works for Carter Lansing who used to have big mob connections in the old days. Now he's going straight and owns most of So-Flo Airways with headquarters in Miami. Two, Benny Quick has left the Miami area for parts unknown. Benny has been showing lots of green lately. Anything else?"

"Yeah. Name Simpson in connection with Nat Paley or Lennie Weaver mean anything?"

"Sure, remember Red Dog Wally? He's got a bookie stall on Forty-ninth . . . other day he mentioned old Pig-face Weaver. Some broad was around looking him up with tears in her eyes. A real looker, he said, but nobody knew a thing about Lennie. Red Dog said he'd ask around, found out that Lenny and Nat had something big going for them with an out of town customer and were playing it cozy. No squeal out on them either. So Red Dog told the broad and she almost broke down."

"Then their client could be Simpson."

"Who knows. Hell, they've strong-armed for big guys from politicians to ladies' underwear manufacturers."

"Okay, Artie, thanks a bunch."

I hung up and stood there a minute, trying to think. I went over the picture twice and picked up an angle. I grinned at the thought and turned around.

She was waiting for me, tall, beautiful, her hair so shiny you wanted to bathe in it. The gentle rise and fall of her breasts said this was a moment she had thought about and planned. She tried a tiny smile and said, "Kelly?"

"Let's keep it Mr. Smith. I don't want to be friendly with the help."

She tried to hold her head up and keep the smile on, but I saw her eyes go wet.

I tipped her chin up. "Now that we've exchanged nasties, everybody's even. Think you can smile again?"

It came back, crookedly at first, but there it was and she was something so damn crazy special I could hardly believe it.

"Mr. Smith . . ."

I took her hand. "Kelly. Let's make it Kelly, sugar."

Before I knew what she was going to do it was over, a kiss, barely touching, but for one fraction of an instant a fierce, restrained moment. We both felt it and under the sheer midnight of her blouse a ripple seemed to touch her shoulder and her breasts went hard.

She went with me, out to the truck, waiting while I went into police headquarters. I asked for Captain Cox and when he came said, "I want to lodge a complaint against two of Mr. Simpson's employees. One is Nat Paley, the other a stranger."

Cox's face drew tight. "About your brawl, I suppose."

"That's right. They attacked me on the street. I recognized Paley and can identify the other by sight."

Nodding, Cox said, "We checked that one through already. The housekeeper whose place you used called us. Another party down the street thought he recognized one of Simpson's cars. However, Mr. Simpson himself said none of his cars was out and all his employees were on the premises. A dozen others can vouch for it."

"I see."

"Anybody else to back up your side?"

I grinned at him. "I think it can be arranged."

"You're causing a lot of trouble, Mister," he told me.

My grin got big enough so he could see all the teeth. "Hell, I haven't even started yet."

Dari and I drove through town and picked up a macadam road leading into the hills. Below us to the right Lake Rappaho was a huge silver puddle. Two lesser roads intersected and joined the one we were on.

At the next bend we came upon the outer defenses of Simpson's place. A sign read Hillside Manor Private. It was set in a fieldstone wall a good 10 feet high and on top were shards of broken glass set in concrete. That wasn't all. Five feet out there was a heavy wire fence with a three-strand barbed wire overhang.

"Nice," I said. "He's really in there. How long has it been like this?"

"Since the war. About '47."

"This guy Simpson . . . he's always had the place?"

"No. There was another. It changed hands about ten years ago. That is, at least the owners changed. But the visitors; they're always the same. You never see them in town at all. They come and go at night or come in by the North Fork Road or by Otter Pass. Sometimes there are a hundred people up there a week or two at a time."

"It can accommodate that many?"

"At least. There are twenty-some rooms in the big house and six outbuildings with full accommodations. It's almost like a huge private club."

"Nobody's ever been nosy enough to look inside?"

After a moment she said, "They caught Jake Adler in there once and beat him up terribly. Captain Cox has been in a couple of times, but said he saw nothing going on. Several years ago two hunters were reported missing in this area. They were found dead a week later . . . fifty miles away. Their car went over a cliff. The police said they had changed their plans and decided to hunt elsewhere."

"Could have been."

"Possibly. Only one of them made a phone call from the hotel the day they were supposed to have disappeared."

I looked at her incredulously. "You report that?"

"They said I wasn't positive enough. I only had a photograph to go on and in brush clothes all hunters tend to look alike."

"Nice. Real nice. How can we get a look in there then?"

"You can see the house from the road a little way up. I don't know how you can get inside though. The wall goes all the way around and down to the lake."

"There's an approach on the water?"

Her forehead creased in thought. "There's a landing there with a path leading through the woods. It's well hidden in a finger cove. Are you . . ."

"Let's see the house first."

We found the spot. I parked the car and stood there at the lip, looking across a quarter-mile gulf of densely wooded valley at the white house that looked like a vacation hotel.

A few figures moved on the lawn and a few more clustered on the porch, their dark clothes marking them against the stark white of the building.

Behind me, Dari said, "A car is coming."

It was a blue sedan, an expensive job, the two in front indiscernible in the shadows. But the New York City plate wasn't. I wrote the number down and didn't bother putting the pencil back. Another plume of dust was showing around the Otter Pass intersection and I waited it out. We were back to black Caddies again and this one had four men in it and upstate New York plates. Fifteen minutes later a white Buick station wagon rolled past and the guy beside the driver was looking my way.

Harry Adrano hadn't changed much in the five years he had been up the river. His face was still set in a perpetual scowl, still blue-black with beard, his mouth a hard slash. And Harry was another number in a crazy combination because wherever Harry went one of the poppy derivatives was sure to follow.

Very softly I said, "Like Apalachin . . . I got to get inside there."

"You can't. The main gate is guarded."

"There's the lake . . ."

"Somebody will be there, too. Why do you have to go inside?"

"Because I want to get the numbers on any cars that are up there."

"You'll get killed in there."

"You know a better way?"

The smile she gave me matched her eyes. "Yes. Grace Shaefer was in town yesterday. She'll be making herself available for the . . . festivities there."

"Do you think she'll go along with that?"

Dari's smile changed. "I figure you'll be able to coax her into it."

"Thanks," I said.

I took her arm and headed for the car. Before we reached it I heard tires digging into the road up ahead and tried to duck back into the brush. It wasn't any good. The black Cad swept by going back toward town and both the guys in it had plenty of time to spot the two of us, if they had bothered to look. It didn't seem that they had, but Benny Quick was driving and that little punk could see all around him without moving his head.

We waited, heard the car fade off downhill, then got in the truck. At the Otter Pass turn-off, fresh tire tracks scarred the dirt and a broken whiskey bottle glinted at the side of the road.

Just beyond the North Fork Road, the road turned sharply, and that's where they were waiting. The Cad was broadside to us and Benny was standing beside it. If we were just casual tourists, it would look like a minor accident, but anything else and it was a neat trap.

I braked to a stop 20 feet short of the Caddy and stuck my head half out the window so the corner post covered most of my face. Benny Quick tried to adjust a pleasant smile to fit his squirrelly expression, but did a lousy job of it.

But Benny wasn't the one I was worried about. Someplace nearby the other guy was staked out and there was a good chance he had a rod in his fist. I tugged the .45 out and thumbed the hammer back. Beside me Dari froze.

I put on the neighborly act, too. "Trouble, friend?"

Benny started toward me. I opened the door of the cab and swung it out as if I were trying to get a better look. I saw Benny take in the Willie Elkins' Garage, Repairs and Towing Call Pinewood 101 sign printed there, make a snap decision, figure us for locals in the woods, and decide to write us off as coincidence.

His smile stretched a little. "No, . . . no trouble. Pulled a little hard on the turn and skidded around. Just didn't want anybody ramming me while I turned around."

He got in the Cad, gunned the engine, and made a big production of jockeying around in the small area. He wound up pointing back toward the mountain and waved as he went by. I waved too and at that moment our eyes met and something seemed to go sour with Benny Quick's grin.

Either he was turning it off as a bad fit a little too fast or he recognized me from a time not so long ago.

Around the bend ahead I stopped suddenly, cut the engine, and listened. Then I heard a door slam and knew Benny had picked up his passenger. Dari was watching me and I didn't have to tell her what had just happened.

Silently, her eyes dropped to the .45 on the seat, then came back to mine. She said, "You would have killed him, wouldn't you?"

"It would have been a pleasure," I said.

"It's terrible," she whispered.

"Well, don't let it snow you, kid. I may have to do it yet."

It was dark when we reached the hotel. The clerk waved Dari over and said, "Right after you left a call came in. Girl said she was Ruth Gleason. She sounded almost hysterical. I couldn't make much out of it. She was crying and talking about needing somebody."

Dari's face turned ashen. She turned to me, waiting. "You said you could reach Grace Shaefer," I reminded her.

Dari nodded.

"See if she can meet us at Jimmie's bar in an hour."

Ten minutes went by before the operator got my call through to Artie. As usual, we made idle talk before I gave him the plate numbers I had picked up on the mountain road. He grunted disgustedly when I told him I wanted it right away. This would take a little time, so I left the number of the hotel and said I'd stand by.

I looked at my watch and told the clerk to put any calls through to me in Dari's room.

Dari's room was on the ground floor at the end of the corridor. I knocked and heard her call for me to come in. I stood there a moment in the semidarkness of the small foyer and then, unlike her, turned the key in the lock. Inside I could hear her talking over the phone.

She was curled up on the end of a studio couch, wrapped in a black and red mandarin robe that had a huge golden dragon embroidered on it. The fanged mouth was at her throat.

She had a Mrs. Finney on the wire. Trying to conceal her annoyance, Dari said, "Well, when Grace does call, can you have her meet me at Jimmie's in an hour? Tell her it's very important. All right. Thanks, Mrs. Finney."

She hung up and grimaced. "She knows where Grace is, damn it."

"Why is it a secret?"

"Because . . ." she gave me an impish grin, "Mrs. Finney's rooming house is . . . a little more than a rooming house. During the summer, that is."

"Oh," I said. "And she's still loyal to her . . . clients?"

"Something like that."

"The national pastime. No place is too big or too little for it. Any town, anyplace, and there's always a Mrs. Finney. Do you think she'll speak to Grace?"

"She'll be there." She stood up, the satiny folds of the robe whipping around her until the golden dragon seemed almost alive.

There is some crazy fascination about a big woman. And when I looked at her I knew that her love was my kind, greedy, wanting to have everything; violent, wanting to give everything. Her eyes seemed to slant up and the front of the robe followed the concavity of her belly as she sucked in her breath. Her breasts were high and firm, their movement making the dragon's head move toward her throat hungrily.

I held out my hand and without hesitation she took it. When I pulled her toward me she came effortlessly, sliding down beside me, leaning back against the cushions with eyes half-slitted to match those of the guardian golden dragon.

My hands slid around her, feeling the heat of her body through the sheen of the satin. There was nothing soft about her. She was hard and vibrant, quivering under my touch and, although she was waiting, she was tensing to spring, too, and I could sense the flexing and rolling of the muscles at her stomach and across her back.

Her fingertips were on me, touching with wary gentleness and having the knowledge of possession, but first exploring the fullness of something she now owned. One hand went behind my head, kneaded my neck, and the other guided my face to hers. No word was spoken. There was need for none. This was the now when everything was known and everything that was to be would be.

She held me away an instant, searching my face, then, realizing how we both desperately hated the silent restraint, did as a woman might and licked my lips with her tongue until they were as wet as her own and with a startled cry let herself explode into a kiss with me that was a wild maelstrom of a minute that seemed to go on endlessly.

My fingers bit into her wrists. "Now you know."

"Now I know," she answered. "It never happened to me before, Kelly."

Dari raised my hands to her mouth, kissed the backs of my hands and smiled.

"What do we do now?" she asked me.

"We don't throw this away, kid. It's ours. We'll take it right and keep it forever."

Slowly she uncoiled, stood in front of me and let all the love in her face tell me I had said what she wanted to hear but didn't expect.

She let me watch her, then laughed deep in her throat and said, "What are you thinking?"

"I'm thinking that you're not wearing anything at all under that . . . geisha thing."

"You're right," she said.

She let me look and hunger another moment, then fingered the clasp of the robe. She held each edge in her hand and threw her arms back slowly, unfolding the robe like immense, startlingly crimson wings, and stood outlined against them in sheer sun-tanned beauty highlighted by the mouth so red and hair so blonde.

With another smile my Valkyrie turned and moved away slowly into the bedroom opposite, and behind me the phone rang so suddenly I jumped.

The desk clerk said, "Mr. Smith, I have your New York call."

My tone stopped Artie's usual kidding around.

"Okay, buddy," he said, "but you got yourself a mixed-up package. Two of those cars, a station wagon and a sedan, belong to businessmen who show clean all the way."

"Maybe, Art, but Harry Adrano was riding in the wagon and that boy's been working with the happy dust."

"That one Cadillac is a rented car. The guy who signed out for it is a Walter Cramer nobody knows anything about, but the guy who paid the tab *is* something. He's Sergei Rudinoff, a Soviet attaché who's been in this country three months."

I thanked Art, hung up, and stared at the phone. The picture was coming through loud and clear.

Dari took me out back to her car and handed me the keys.

It was 8:30. Jimmie spotted us when we walked in and came down.

"Grace Shaefer's in the back. Said she's waiting for you."

I grinned back and we headed for the back room.

Grace Shaefer sat there nursing a highball. She was a wide-eyed brunette with a voluptuously full body in no way disguised by the black, low-cut dress. The white swell of her breasts was deliberately flaunted, the outline of her crossed legs purposely apparent. One time she had been beautiful, but now her beauty had gone down the channels of whoredom.

"Hello, Dari. Who's your big friend?"

"This is Kelly Smith. How have you been, Grace?"

Her smile was to me, a plain invitation, though she spoke to Dari. "I've been fine. Let's say, I have everything I've ever wanted."

"Grace . . . are you going up on the hill this time?"

"Yes, I am," she said, almost defiantly. "Why?"

Before Dari could answer I said, "How thick are you involved, Grace?"

"Say, look . . ."

"You're hooked, baby. You can get out of it if you want to."

There was genuine fear in her eyes. "I got the feeling you're looking to get yourself killed," she told me.

"It's been tried. Now . . . how about you? If you want, you can do me a favor up there."

When she answered I knew she had made up her mind. She said, "Smithy boy, like you know my kind, I know yours. Let's not turn our backs on ourselves. The day I want to commit suicide I'll do you a favor, otherwise from now on stay clear of me. That plain?"

I nodded. But Grace wasn't finished yet. With that subtle intuition some people have, she knew what was between us and said to Dari, "I could do you a favor though, Dari. Mr. Simpson is having a party tonight. He could do with more girls. One thing a pretty bitch like you can be sure of, you'll always be welcome up there. Just come willingly. Remember?"

I grabbed Dari's arm before she could hit her and with a deliberate smirk Grace tossed her furs over her shoulders and walked out.

The outside door slammed open. The kid who came in was scared and out of breath. He gasped and said, "Mr. Smith . . ."

Then I recognized him. Sonny Holmes, the one who braced Paley and Weaver in the bar over the Evans girl.

"Mr. Smith . . . they're looking for you. I'm telling you, they're after you bad."

I grabbed his shoulder. "Who?"

"Those two you fought with because of me. They were over at your hotel asking for you and the desk clerk said you'd be here."

"Those two don't bother me."

"Maybe not them, but they went outside and talked to some others in a car. A Cadillac from the hill."

"Benny Quick spotted me. That little bastard finally got his memory back. Well, the next time I tag him he won't have any memory left." My voice came through my teeth.

"Mr. Smith, you better get out of here."

Without knowing it, I had the .45 in my hand.

"Look, kid, you take Miss Dahl out of here. Get in her car and make sure you're not followed. Try to get to the police. You tell Cox his town is about to explode."

"No, Kelly . . ."

"Don't start bugging me now, Dari. Do what you're told. This is my kind of business and I'll take care of it my way."

She glanced at the gun. "That's what I'm afraid of. Kelly . . . don't let's spoil it so quickly, please, Kelly." She paused, her eyes wet. "You've been one of them. I think everybody knew it. You carry a gun . . . you've been shot . . . you're here in the middle of all this. Run, darling . . . please. I don't care what you were, don't stay part of this or they'll kill you!"

"Not while I have a rod, kitten."

Her words sounded flat. "That's just as bad, isn't it?" she asked. "You kill them . . . and the law kills you."

I could feel the amazement in the short laugh I let out. I cut it off, grinned, and handed her the .45. "Okay, kitten, have it your way."

She dropped the gun in her pocket, went to kiss me, and then everything out in the bar went quiet. Before she could move, I shoved her in Sonny's arms and whispered harshly, "Take her, damn it!"

When the door closed behind them I turned, ran to the

bank of windows at the side of the room, and felt for the catch. Slowly, a drop of sweat trickled down my back. The windows were the steel casement awning type and somebody had removed the crank handles. Another second and they'd be back here and there wasn't time to break out.

At the end of the room were the johns and on a sudden thought I turned into the one marked WOMEN. If they searched the place they'd go to the other one first instinctively. There was no lock on the outside door, but a waste basket fitted under the knob. Another couple of seconds maybe. The window there was the same as the others, steel casement with the handle gone. It was shoulder high and the opaque, wire-impregnated glass was practically unbreakable.

Outside, I heard muffled voices. I cursed softly, fighting the stem of the window handle. It wouldn't budge. I reached back, grabbed a handful of paper, and wrapped a section around the toothed edges. This time when I twisted, the stem gave a little. With exasperating slowness the window began to swing out. On the other side of the wall a heavy foot kicked the door open and somebody said, "Come on out of there!"

If the men's room was the same as this, they could see the shut window and know I didn't go out it, but they couldn't see into the closed toilet booth and would figure I was holed up there. I grinned, thinking that it was a hell of a place to be trapped.

The window was out far enough then. I hauled myself up, squirmed through the opening as a hand tried the door.

Under me was a driveway. One end was blocked by a building, the other was open into the lighted street. I ran toward the light and was a second too late because somebody cut the corner sharply and I could see the gun in his fist.

But the edge was still mine. He had not yet adjusted to the deep black of the alley, and for me he was a lovely silhouette. He could hear my feet and raised the gun. Before he could pull the trigger I crossed one into his jaw that took bone and teeth with it and he hit the ground as if he were dead and I spilled on my face across him.

The other guy was on top of me before I could get up. I dove for the gun the first guy had dropped, fumbled it, and the other one had me.

He should have shot me and been done with it. Instead he cut loose with a running kick that seemed to splinter into my bad side like I had lain on a grenade. It was the amazing agony of the kick that saved me. I arched away from the next one with a tremendous burst of energy and my spasmodic kick spilled the guy on top of me.

I had the other gun then. Grabbing it was instinctive. Slamming it against his ear was instinctive.

Never before had the bulging fire in my side been like this, not even when it happened. I tried to wish myself unconscious . . . anything to get away from it. And instinctively I realized that the only thing that would stop it was up in my room at the hotel.

Then it's over and you don't know how it happened. You don't remember the route, the obstacles, the staircase. You can almost forget instinct as you open the door, then it's there again, because the door should have been locked and you throw yourself on the floor as a little bright flash of light winks in the darkness. Getting the gun up is instinctive and as something tugs into the flesh of your upper arm you put out the light that has been trying to kill you.

A few feet away something crumples to the floor and you get up, flip the switch, and see Benny Quick lying face up with a hole between his eyes.

I didn't waste time. I shook out six capsules and washed them down. For a minute I stood there, waiting for the relief to come. And gently it came, like a wave of soft warm water, so that once more I could think and act like a person instead of an instinct-led animal.

They were looking for me on the street. They'd come here next to check with Benny. They'd find Benny dead and the big hunt would be on. My mind was fuzzy now. I shoved the gun under my belt, stuck Benny's in my pocket, and got my hands under his arms. Benny had died quickly. A scatter rug covered the signs of his final exit and I dragged him outside, closing the door after me.

I could think of only one place to put him. I got him down the back stairs and around the corner to the door of Dari's room. I dragged the body in and dumped it on the floor because it was as far as I could go with it.

Across the room a girl was trying to scream. She watched me with eyes so black they seemed unreal and when she got done trying to scream she collapsed on the floor.

The girl began to sob. I knew who she was. Tentatively, I said, "Ruth? Ruth Gleason?"

She seemed to realize that I wouldn't hurt her. The glazed look left her eyes and she got her feet under her. "Y-yes."

"Dari . . . have you see Dari?"

"No . . . I tried to . . . I waited . . ."

Think, I thought, *damn it, THINK!*

The Holmes kid would have taken her somewhere. Dr. McKeever had the Evans girl at his wife's sister's place. The kid would go there.

"Would you know Dr. McKeever's wife . . . or her sister?" I asked.

For a second Ruth Gleason stopped being scared and bobbed her head, puzzled. "Her sister is Emma Cox . . . Captain Cox's wife. They . . . don't live together anymore."

"Can you drive?"

She nodded again. I reached in my pocket and threw her the truck keys. "Willie Elkins' truck. It's out back. You call Doctor McKeever and tell him to meet us at his sister's. You'll have to drive."

I could hear her voice but couldn't concentrate on it. I felt her hand on my arm and knew I was in the truck. I could smell the night air and sometimes think and cursed myself mentally for having gone overboard with those damned capsules.

Time had no meaning at all. I heard Dr. McKeever and Dari and felt hands in the hole in my side and knew pieces of flesh were being cut away from the hole in my arm. There was Dari crying and the Gleason girl screaming.

All she could say was, "You're a doctor, give it to me, please. You have to! Oh, please . . . I'll do anything . . . please!"

Dari said, "Can you . . . ?"

There were other voices and McKeever finally said, "It'll help. Not much, but it will quiet her."

"And Kelly?" she asked.

"He'll be all right. I'll have to report this gunshot wound."

"No." There was a soft final note in her voice. "He has to get away."

Ruth Gleason was crying out for Lennie to please come get her.

The pain-killing fog I was wrapped in detached me from the scene then.

"You've been withdrawing, haven't you, Ruth?" Dr. McKeever asked.

Her voice was resigned. "I didn't want to. Lennie . . . took it away. He wanted to . . . get rid of me."

After a moment McKeever continued, "When did it start, Ruth?"

Her voice sounded real distant. "On the hill. Flori and I . . . went there. Flori needed the money . . . her father . . ."

"Yes, I know about that. What about you?"

"A man . . . before Lennie. We met downtown and he . . . invited me. It sounded like fun. He gave me some pot."

Dari said, "What?"

"Marihuana," the doctor told her. "Then what, Ruth?"

"Later we popped one. For kicks. Week later."

"Flori, too?"

Ruth giggled. "Sure," she said, "everybody. It was fun. He danced. Nude, you know? No clothes. Mr. Simpson came in and watched. He gave me five hundred dollars, can you imagine? Flori too. And that was only the first time. Oh, we did lots of dances. We wore costumes for Mr. Simpson and we made his friends laugh and we . . ."

You could barely hear her voice. "Mr. Simpson wanted . . . something special. On different nights . . . he'd take one of us. He made us undress . . . and he had whips.

He said . . . it wouldn't hurt." She almost choked, remembering. "I screamed and tried to get away, but I couldn't!" She buried her face in her hands.

"You went back, Ruth?"

"I . . . had to. The money. It was always there. Then there was Lennie. Then I had to because . . . my supply was gone . . . I needed a shot bad. I . . . what's going to happen to me?"

"You'll be taken care of, Ruth. Tell me something . . . are any girls up there now?"

"Yes . . . yes. The ones who are usually there. But there will be more. Mr. Simpson likes . . . new ones. Please . . . you'll have to let me go back."

The voices were miles away now. Sleep was pressing down on me and I couldn't fight it off.

It was daylight. I cursed and yelled for somebody and the door opened and McKeever was trying to push me back on the cot. Behind him was Sonny Holmes.

I managed to sit up against the pressure of McKeever's hand. My mouth was dry and cottony, my head pounding. A tight band of wide tape was wound around my torso and the pain in my side was a dull throbbing, but it was worse than the hole in the fleshy part of my arm.

"I haven't seen anything like you since the war," McKeever said.

From the door Cox said, "Can he talk?"

Before McKeever could stop me I said, "I can talk, Captain. Come on in."

Cox's arrogant smile was gone now. Like everybody else in Pinewood, he had a nervous mouth.

I said, "I made you big trouble, boy, didn't I?"

"You had no right . . ."

"Tough. You checked my prints through, didn't you?"

He couldn't hide the fear in his eyes. McKeever was watching me too now. "I'm a federal agent, laddie, and you know it. At any time my department has authority to operate anywhere and by now you know with what cooperation, don't you?"

Cox didn't answer. He was watching his whole little world come tumbling down around him.

"You let a town run dirty, Cox. You let a worm get in a long time ago and eat itself into a monster. The worm got too big, so you tried to ignore it and you played a mutual game of Let Alone. It outgrew you, buddy. I bet you've known that for a long, long time. Me happening along was just an accident, but it would have caught up to you before long anyway."

Cox still wouldn't put his head down. "What should I do," he asked.

I got up on the edge of the bed, reached for my pants, and pulled them on. Somebody had washed my shirt. Luckily, I could slide my feet into my moccasins without bending down.

I looked hard at the big cop. "You'll do nothing," I said. "You'll go back to your office and wait there until I call and tell you what to do. Now get out of here."

We both watched Cox shuffle out. His head was down a little now. McKeever said, "Can you tell me?"

I nodded. "I have to. If anything happens to me, you'll have to pass it on. Now I'm going to guess, but it won't be wild. That big house on the hill is a front, a meeting place for the grand brotherhood of the poppy.

"It isn't the only one they have . . . it's probably just a local chapter. It's existed, operated, and been successful for . . . is it ten years now? Down here, the people maybe even suspected. But who wants to play with mob boys? It wouldn't take much to shut mouths up down here. To make it even better, that bunch spread the loot around. Even the dolls could be hooked into the action and nobody would really beef. Fear and money were a powerful deterrent. Besides, who could they beef to? A cop scared to lose his job? And other cops scared of him?

"But one day the situation changed. Overseas imports of narcotics had been belted by our agencies and the brotherhood was hurting. But timed just right was the Cuban deal and those slobs on the hill got taken in by the Reds who saw a way of injecting a poison into this country while they built up their own machine. So Cuba became a collection point for China-grown narcotics. There's a supposedly clean businessman up there on the hill who owns an airline in Florida. The connection clear?"

I grinned, my teeth tight. "There's an even bigger one there, a Russian attaché. He'll be the one who knows where and when the big delivery will be made. There's a rallying of key personnel who have to come out of hiding in order to attend a conclave of big wheels and determine short-range policy.

"It's a chance they have to take. You can't be in the business they're in without expecting to take a chance sooner or later. Lack of coincidence can eliminate chance. Coincidence can provide it. I was the coincidence. Only there was another element involved . . . a Mr. Simpson and his peculiar pleasures. If he had forgone those, chance never would have occurred."

It was a lot of talk. It took too damn much out of me. I said, "Where's Dari?"

The doctor was hesitant until I grabbed his arm. When he looked up his face was drained of color. "She went after Ruth."

My fingers tightened and he winced. "I put Ruth . . . to bed. What I gave her didn't hold. She got up and left. The next morning, Dari left too."

"What are you talking about . . . *the next morning?*"

"You took a big dosage, son. That was yesterday. You've been out all this time."

It was like being hit in the stomach.

I stood up and pulled on my jacket.

The doctor said, "They're all over town. They're waiting for you."

"Good," I said. "Where's Sonny Holmes?"

"In the kitchen."

From Sonny's face, I knew he had heard everything we had said. I asked him, "You know how to get to the lake without going through town?"

Sonny had changed. He seemed older. "There's a way. We can take the old icecart trail to the lake."

I grinned at the doctor and handed him a card. "Call that number and ask for Artie. You tell him the whole thing, but tell him to get his tail up here in a hurry. I'm going to cut Dari out of this deal, doc." The look on his face stopped me.

"She's gone," he said. "She went up there as guest.

. . . She said something about Ruth Gleason saying they wanted girls. She had a gun in her pocketbook. She said it was yours. Kelly . . . she went up there to kill Simpson! She went alone. She said she knew how she could do it . . ."

And that was a whole day ago.

Sonny was waiting. We used his car. My rented truck was gone. Ruth Gleason had taken it and the silenced gun I had used was in it.

Mort Steiger said, "I was waiting for you."

"No fishing, pop," I told him.

"I know what you're going to do. I knew it all along. Somebody had to. You looked like the only one who could and who wanted to."

I turned to Sonny. "Call the doc, kid. See if he got through to my friend."

Mort held out his hand and stopped him. "No use trying. The phones are all out. The jeep from the hill run into a pole down by the station and it'll be two days before a repair crew gets here."

"Sonny," I said, "you get back to Captain Cox. You tell him I'm going inside and to get there with all he has. Tell him they're my orders."

Mort spit out the stub of a cigar. "I figured you right, I did. You're a cop, ain't you?"

I looked at him and grinned. My boat was still there where I had left it. The sun was sinking.

The guy on the dock died easily and quietly. He tried to go for his gun when he saw me and I took him with one sudden stroke. The one at the end in the neat gray suit who looked so incongruous holding a shotgun went just as easily.

An eighth of a mile ahead, the roof of the house showed above the trees. When I reached the main building I went in through the back. It was dark enough now so that I could take advantage of shadows. Above me the house was brilliantly lit. There was noise and laughter and the sound of music and women's voices and the heavier voices of men.

There could only be a single direct line to the target. I

nailed a girl in toreador pants trying to get ice out of the freezer. She had been around a long time, maybe not in years, but in time you can't measure on a calendar. She knew she was standing an inch from dying and when I said, "Where is Simpson?" she didn't try to cry out or lie or anything else.

She simply said, "The top floor," and waited for what she knew I'd do to her. I sat her in a chair, her feet tucked under her. For an hour she'd be that way, passed out to any who noticed her.

It was another 20 minutes before I had the complete layout of the downstairs.

What got me was the atmosphere of the place. It was too damn gay. It took a while, but I finally got it. The work had been done, the decisions made, and now it was time to relax.

My stomach went cold and I was afraid of what I was going to find.

It didn't take any time to reach the top floor. Up here you couldn't hear the voices nor get the heavy smell of cigar smoke. I stood on the landing looking toward the far end where the corridor opened on to two doors. To the left could be only small rooms because the corridor was so near the side of the building. To the right, I thought, must be almost a duplicate of the big room downstairs.

And there I was. What could I do about it? Nothing.

The gun in my back said nothing.

Lennie Weaver said, "Hello, jerk."

Behind Lennie somebody said, "Who is he, Len?"

"A small-time punk who's been trying to get ahead in the business for quite a while now. He didn't know what he was bucking." The gun nudged me again. "Keep going, punk. Last door on your left. You open it, you go in, you move easy, or that's it."

The guy said, "What's he doing here?"

I heard Lennie laugh. "He's nuts. Remember what he pulled on Nat and me? They'll try anything to get big time. He's the fink who ran with Benny Quick and turned him in to the fuzz."

We came to the door and went inside and stood there until the tremendously fat man at the desk finished writing. When he looked up, Lennie said, "Mr. Simpson, here's the guy who was causing all the trouble in town."

And there was Mr. Simpson. Mr. Simpson who only went as far as his middle name in this operation. Mr. Simpson by his right name, everybody would know. They would remember the recent election conventions or recall the five percenters and the political scandals a regime ago. Hell, everybody would know Mr. Simpson by his whole name.

The fleshy moon face was blank. The eyes blinked and the mouth said, "You know who he is?"

"Sure." Lennie's laugh was grating. "Al Braddock. Like Benny Quick said, he picked up something some place and tried to build into it. He wouldn't have sounded off, Mr. Simpson. He'd want any in with us for himself. Besides, who'd play along? They know what happens.

"What shall we do with him, Mr. Simpson?" Lennie asked.

Simpson almost smiled. "Why just kill him, Lennie," he said and went back to the account book.

It was to be a quiet affair, my death. My hands were tied behind me and I was walked to the yard behind the building.

"Why does a punk like you want in for?" Lennie asked. "How come you treat life the way you do?"

"The dame, pal," I said. "I got a yen for a dame."

"Who?" His voice was unbelieving.

"Dari Dahl. She inside?"

"You are crazy, buddy," he told me. "Real nuts. In ten minutes that beautiful broad of yours goes into her act and when she's done she'll never be the same. She'll make a cool grand up there, but man, she's had it. I know the kind it makes and the kind it breaks. That mouse of yours won't have enough spunk left to puke when she walks out of there." He laughed again. "If she walks. She may get a ride back to the lights, if she wants to avoid her friends. A guy up there is willing to take second smacks on her anytime."

"Too bad," I said. "If it's over, it's over. Like your two friends down at the lake."

Lennie said, "What?"

"I knocked off two guys by the lake."

The little guy got the point quickly. "Hell, he didn't come in over the wall, Len. He came by the path. Jeeze, if the boss knows about that, he'll fry. The whole end is open, if he's right."

But Lennie wasn't going to be taken. "Knock it off, Moe. We'll find him out. We'll go down that way. If he's right or wrong, we'll still fix him. Hell, it could even be fun. We'll drown the bastard."

"You watch it, Len; this guy's smart."

"Not with two guns in his back and his hands tied, he's not." His mouth twisted. "Walk, punk."

Time, time. Any time, every time. Time was life. Time was Dari. If you had time, you could think and plan and move.

Then time was bought for me.

From somewhere in the darkness Ruth Gleason came running, saying, "Lennie, Lennie . . . don't do this to me, please!" and threw herself at the guy.

He mouthed a curse and I heard him hit her, an open-handed smash that knocked her into the grass. "Damn these whores, you can't get them off your back!"

Ruth sobbed, tried to get up, her words nearly inaudible. "Please Lennie . . . they won't give me . . . anything. They laughed and . . . threw me out."

I just stood there. Any move I made would get me a bullet so I just stood there. I could see Ruth get to her feet and stagger, her body shaking. She held on to a stick he had picked up. I could see the tears on her cheeks.

"Lennie . . . I'll do anything. Anything. Please . . . you said you loved me. Tell them to get me a fix."

Lennie said two words.

They were his last.

With unexpected suddenness she ran at him, that stick in her hands, and I saw her lunge forward with it and the thing sink into Lennie's middle like a broken sword and heard his horrible rattle. It snapped in her hands with a foot of it inside him and he fell, dying, while she clawed at him with maniacal frenzy.

The other guy ran for her, tried to pull her off, and

forgot about me. My hands were tied. My feet weren't. It took only three kicks to kill him.

Ruth still beat at the body, not realizing Lennie was dead.

"Ruth . . . I can get you a fix!" I said.

The words stopped her. She looked at me, not quite seeing me. "You can?"

"Untie me. Hurry."

I turned around and felt her fingers fumble with the knots at my wrists until they fell free.

"Now . . . you'll get me a fix? Please?"

I nodded and hit her. Later she could get her fix. Maybe she'd made it so she'd never need one again. Later was lots of things, but she'd bought my time for me and I wouldn't forget her.

The little guy's gun was a .32 and I didn't want it. I liked Lennie's .45 better, and it fitted my hand like a glove. My forefinger found the familiar notch in the butt and I knew I had my own gun back and knew the full implication of Lennie's words about Dari.

She had tried for her kill and missed. Somebody else got the gun and Dari was to get the payoff.

This time I thought it out. I knew how I had to work it. I walked another 100 yards to the body of the gray-suited guard I had left earlier, took his shotgun from the ground and four extra shells from his pocket, and started back to the house.

Nothing had changed. Downstairs they were still drinking and laughing, still secure.

I found the 1,500-gallon fuel tank above ground as I expected, broke the half-inch copper tubing, and let the oil run into the whiskey bottles I culled from the refuse dump. It didn't take too many trips to wet down the bushes around the house. They were already season-dried, the leaves crisp. A huge puddle had run out from the line, following the contour of the hill and running down the drive to the front of the house.

It was all I needed. I took two bottles, filled them, and tore off a hunk of my shirt tail for a wick. Those bottles would make a high flash-point Molotov cocktail, if I could keep them lit. The secret lay in a long wick so the fuel oil, spilling out, wouldn't douse the flame. Not as good as gasoline, but it would do.

Then I was ready.

Nothing fast. The normal things are reassuring. I coughed, sniffed, and reached the landing at the first floor. When the man there saw me he tried to call out and died before he could. The other one was just as unsuspecting. He died just as easily. Soft neck.

Mr. Simpson's office was empty. I opened his window, lit my wick on the whiskey bottle, and threw it down. Below me there was a small breaking of glass, a tiny flame that grew. I drew back from the window.

I had three more quarts of fuel oil under my arm. I let it run out at the two big doors opposite Simpson's office and soak into the carpet. This one caught quickly, a sheet of flame coming off the floor. Nobody was coming out that door.

Some place below there was a yell, then a scream. I opened the window and got out on the top of the second floor porch roof. From there the top floor was blanked out completely. Heavy drapes covered the windows and, though several were open for ventilation, not a streak of light shone through.

I stepped between the window and the draperies, entirely concealed, then held the folds of the heavy velvet back. It was a small theatre in the round. There was a person shrouded in black tapping drums and that was all the music they had. Two more in black tights with masked faces were circling about a table. They each held long thin whips, and whenever the drummer raised the tempo they snapped them, and sometimes simply brought them against the floor so that the metal tips made a sharp popping sound.

She was there in the middle, tied to the table. She was robed in a great swath of silk.

From where I stood I could see the town and the long line of lights winding with tantalizing slowness toward the hill.

Down below they were yelling now, their voices frantic, but here in this room nobody was listening. They were watching the performance, in each one's hand a slim length of belt that could bring joy to minds who had tried everything else and now needed this.

She was conscious. Tied and gagged, but she could know what was happening. She faced the ring of them and saw the curtain move where I was. I took the big chance and moved it enough so she alone could see me standing there and when she jerked her head to keep any-one from seeing the hope in her eyes I knew it was the time.

There was only one other door in the room, a single door on the other side. It was against all fire regulations and now they'd know why. I lit the wick on the last bot-tle, let it catch hold all the way, stepped inside, and threw it across the room.

Everything seemed to come at once . . . the screams, the yelling from outside. Somebody shouted and opened the big doors at the head of the room and a sheet of flame leaped in on the draft.

There was Harry Adrano. I shot him.

There was Calvin Bock. I shot him.

There was Sergei Rudinoff. I shot him and took the briefcase off his body and knew that what I had done would upset the Soviet world.

There was the man who owned the airlines and I shot him.

Only Nat Paley saw me and tried to go for his gun. All the rest were screaming and trying to go through the maze of flame at the door. But it was like Nat to go for his gun so I shot him, too, but not as cleanly as the rest. He could burn the rest of the way.

I got Dari out of the straps that held her down, carried her to the one window that offered escape, and shoved her out. In the room the bongo drummer went scream-ing through the wall of flame. From far off came staccato bursts of gunfire and now no matter what happened, it was won.

I shoved her on the roof and, although everything else was flame, this one place was still empty and cool.

And while she waited for me there, I stepped back in-side the room, the shrivelling heat beating at my face, and saw the gross Mr. Simpson still alive, trapped by his own obesity, a foul thing on a ridiculous throne, still in his robes, still cluthing his belt . . .

And I did him a favor. I said, "So long, Senator."

I brought the shotgun up and let him look all the way into that great black eye and then blew his head off.

It was an easy jump to the ground. I caught her. We walked away.

Tomorrow there would be strange events, strange people, and a new national policy.

But now Dari was looking at me, her eyes loving, her mouth wanting, her mind a turbulence of fear because she thought I was part of it all and didn't know I was a cop, and I had all the time in the world to tell her true.

THE SEVEN YEAR KILL

For seven long years Rocca had been down. And he was almost out when the beautiful brunette wound up in his closet—and started him on a trip that would lead through a terrifying maze of bodies both hot and cold. At the end of the road lay the biggest surprise of all—a surprise that could prove fatal to an ordinary guy.

From far off in the heat and sea of sweat I heard the noise and the voices.

The gloom of the room was split by a shaft of light that stretched across my face from the partly opened door. It was from there that the voice kept saying, "Open this damn door, buddy."

I rolled off the cot and finally got to the door, pushed it shut, slipped off the chain, then backed off when it almost knocked me down swinging open.

Both the hoods were big. The snub-nose jobs in their hands made them even bigger. But they didn't come *that* big. I said, "What the hell you want?"

Without even looking, one swung and last night came boiling out of me all over the floor and I crouched there on my hands and knees trying to keep from dying.

The other guy said, "She ain't here. This joker was drunk on the cot with the chain on. How could she get in here?"

Neither one said anything, but when I raised my head the guy with the long face and bloody shoe was looking at me. I started to grin at him. Not mean. Just a big, friendly grin like I knew how it was and I kept it going until the guy shrugged and said to the other. "He's nuts. Come on."

It was five minutes before I could get up, and another five before I could reach the sink. I ran it cold and splashed it over my face and head, washing the blood down the drain.

I didn't bother looking in the mirror. I felt my way back inside, reached the cot, and flopped out on it, suddenly grateful for the heat of the wall that sucked at the vast pain that was my head.

When I knew I was ready I said, "Okay, come on out of there."

Across the room the panelled closet door that seemed to be part of the wall swung open. For a moment there was only the darkness, then a shadow detached itself from the deeper black, took a step forward with a harsh, shuddering sob, and stood there, rigid.

I reached behind me and turned on the night lamp. It gave off a dull reddish glow, but it was enough.

She was beautiful. There was something Indian-like about her, maybe the black hair or the high planes of her face. Sweat had plastered her dress across her body, her breasts in high, bold relief, the muscular flatness of her belly moving as she breathed. Sudden fear of the hunted had drained her face so that her lips made a full red splash in contrast.

She stood there watching me, saying nothing, a quiver in her flanks as in a mare about to bolt. Spraddle-legged like that I could see the sweep of her thighs and liked what I saw.

I said, "They're gone."

"I never chain that door," I said. "Never. And that closet's the only place to hide in here. Cleverly made, that."

Her tongue flicked out and wet her lips. "When did you . . . realize."

"Right away." The words had blood on them and I wiped it away with my sleeve.

She was staring at my face. "You could have told. Then they . . ."

"I wouldn't tell them punks if their legs were on fire."

"Thank you."

"Sure. It's just a helluva way to get waked up, that's all."

For the first time she started to smile. No, not quite smile . . . a grin, sort of. It changed her whole face and somehow there was no heat and no hangover and no pain in my head and everything was different and I was different. But it was like a flash flood, suddenly there and suddenly gone, leaving behind it only damage from another broken memory.

"Can I do anything for you?"

"Nobody can do anything for me, kid."

She looked around, the grin gone now. "I . . . was running. This was the first place I came to. Your door was open."

I shaded the light with my hand. "Who were they?"

The fear touched her eyes. "I don't know," she finally said.

"They weren't just playing around, kid."

She nodded as if it were a familiar thing to her, then she took a few quick steps across the room and looked over me through the window to the street below.

Close now, I could see she was more lovely than I realized, bigger, and more scared. She was intent on the street below, and when I slipped my hand around hers and squeezed it; she squeezed back involuntarily without realizing it until I let go. Then she gave a sudden start and stepped back quickly, a frown crossing her face.

"I just kissed you," I said.

"What?" softly.

"When we were kids we called it sneak kissing, hand

kissing. It meant you wanted to do more but somebody might be looking." I laughed at the expression on her face, but it hurt my head and I stopped. But it was worth it. I saw the trace of the grin again before the fear came back.

Once more she scanned the street, then said, "I'll have to go now."

"You're crazy if you do. You didn't know those two. How will you know any others who make a try for you. And right now you're a beautiful, sweaty, wet target. In this neighborhood you couldn't be missed."

She sucked her breath in through her teeth, and moved back from the window. I pointed to the chair at the foot of the couch and she sat down, hugging herself as though she were cold.

"When did it happen before?" I asked.

For a moment she stared past me, then shook her head. "I . . . don't know what you mean."

I bit the words out. "You're lying."

The anger came slowly, her folded arms pushing her breasts taut. "Why am I, then?"

"If you didn't know them and didn't expect them to hit, they would have nailed you. They were pros."

The anger receded and it was like losing her outer defenses. I had made her think and correlate and whatever the answers were put her on edge like a great big animal. "All right. It had happened before. Twice."

"When?"

"Tuesday. A car almost ran me down in front of my house. Then the day before yesterday I was followed."

"How'd you know? Pros aren't easy to spot."

Without hesitating she said, "I shopped in the lingerie department of three stores. You don't see many men there and when you do they're noticeable and uncomfortable. I saw this particular one in all three places. I left, made two cab changes, and went into the subway."

She paused, took a deep shuddering breath. Then with a small choking sob, buried her face in her hands and tried to keep from screaming.

I pushed myself up from the cot, my head a sudden spinning ball of pain. I reached over and took her hands down. She wasn't hysterical. She was just on the deep edge momentarily and now she was coming out of it. "Say it," I told her.

She nodded. "The train was coming in the station."

"Go on."

"I . . . felt his hands at my back and he pushed and I was falling and that train was coming on and I could hear the screams and the yells and the train trying to stop and my head hit something and it was like falling into a blessed sleep." She closed her eyes, rubbing at her temples to ease the pain of the thought. "I woke up and they were still yelling and hammering and lights were like fingers poking at me and I didn't know where I was. Terrible. It was terrible."

Then it was my turn to remember. "I saw the pictures. You fell between the tracks in the drainage well. Contusions and abrasions."

"I was very lucky."

"You told them you slipped off the edge."

"I know."

"Why?"

"Some silly woman said I tried to kill myself. She said I jumped. I explained that when I felt myself go I did launch myself out to fall between the tracks."

"They accepted it?"

"Yes. Otherwise I would have been held for observation."

"Smart thinking. Why didn't you say you were pushed?"

She looked up slowly. "I . . . was afraid. It isn't always easy to do certain things when you're afraid."

"Yeah," I said. "I know. What name did you give out?"

"Ann Lowry," she told me, and her eyes were squinting now. "You're asking an awful lot of questions about me. Who are you?"

"Phil Rocca, kid. I'm a nothing."

When a long moment had gone by, she asked quietly, "All right, then. Who *were* you?"

All of it came back like a breath of fresh air. The old days. The long time ago. The quick excitement of life and the feeling of accomplishment. The spicy competition that was in reality a constant war of nerves with all the intrigue and action of actual conflict. Then maybe Rooney's or Patty's for supper, to gloat or sulk depending on who won.

I said, "I was a police reporter on a now defunct journal, a guy who once had a great story. But an editor and a publisher were too cowardly to print it and because I had it I had to be removed. So I was framed into prison. Nobody went to bat for me. I took seven years in the can and the paper and the story is no more. So here I am."

"I'm sorry. Who did a thing like that?"

"A guy I dream about killing every day but never will be able to because he's already dead."

She took in the squalor of the room. "Does it have to be this way?"

"Uh-huh. It does. This is all there is, there ain't no more. Not for me. And as for you, kid, there's only one question more. The BIG WHY. Somebody's trying to finger you out, and the last time they're playing guns. It doesn't get that big without a reason. You're a money dame with money clothes and you wind up in the tenement district in front of two guns. Where were you headed?"

She had to tell somebody. Some things are just too big to hold in long. "I was going to meet my father. I had . . . never seen him."

"Meet him here? In this neighborhood!"

"It was his idea. I think it was because . . . he was down and out. Not that it would have mattered. All my life he took good care of me and my mother. He set up a trust fund for us both even before I was born."

"Why didn't you ever see him?"

"Mother divorced him a year after they were married. She took me to California and never returned. She died there two months ago."

"I'm sorry."

Her shrug was peculiar. "Perhaps I should be too. I'm not. Mother was strange. She was always wrapped up in herself, and her ailments with nothing left over for anybody else, not even me. She would never speak to me about my father. It was as if he had never even existed. If it weren't that I found some of her private papers, I'd never have known what my real name was."

"Oh? What was it?"

She squinted again. "Massley. Terry Massley."

That terrible thing in my stomach uncoiled and pulled at my intestines up into the hollow. I seemed to glow from the sudden flush of blood that a heart gone suddenly berserk threw at a mad pace into the far reaches of its system.

I was so tight and eager again it almost made me sick. I got up, made another trip back to the sink, and ran the bowl brim full with cold water, washed down, and soaked my head clear. Then when the pounding had stopped I pulled in a deep breath and looked at myself in the mirror. Dirty, unshaven, eyes red with too much whiskey and not enough sleep, cheekbones prominent from not enough to eat. And I could smell myself. I stank. But in a way I felt good.

Over my shoulder I saw *her*. Woman-big and beautiful. Her name was Terry Massley.

And Rhino Massley was the guy who had me socked away for seven years.

Rhino had been a smart mobster with millions in loot. He was supposed to be dead, but things like that could be arranged, especially when you have millions.

And now Terry Massley was going to meet her father and, from the kill bits that had been pulled, there was mob action going on and that pointed to a big, wonderful possibility.

Rhino was alive and I could kill him myself!

I stared at my eyes, watching them change. Coincidence, I thought, ah, sweet, lovely coincidence. How I've cursed you and scorned you and declaimed you in the name of objective news reporting. And here you are now knocking at my door. Thanks. Thanks a bunch.

She was puzzled. "Do you feel all right?"

"I feel great," I said. "Would you like me to help you find your father. Coming from the coast you don't know anyone else, do you?"

She shook her head.

"Okay, I know the neighborhood. I'm part of this sewer life and I can move around. I even know tricks that could make me king of this garbage heap, if I wanted it. If your old man is here, I'll find him for you. I'll be glad to. You'll never know how glad I'll be to do it."

She didn't move quickly at all. It was with a deliberate slowness as if she were afraid of herself. She stood up, took a step toward me and slowly sank to her knees. Then she reached up and took my head between her hands and her mouth was a sudden wild, wet fire I had never tasted before and was burning a madness into me I had never wanted to feel again.

I pushed her away and looked at her closely. There was no lie in what she was saying to me. She was saying thanks because I was going to help her find her father.

But I had to be sure. After all this time I couldn't afford to lose a chance at what I wanted by taking one.

I said, "What brought you to this neighborhood to start with?"

The letter she handed me had been typewritten, addressed to her Los Angeles home.

It read:

Dear Terry,

I have just learned of your mother's death. Although we have never met, it is imperative we do so now. Take your mother's personal effects with you and stay at the Sherman the week of the 9th. I will contact you there.

Your Father

"He didn't even sign his name," I said.

"I know. Businessmen do that when their secretary isn't around."

"This isn't the neighborhood to meet businessmen with secretaries," I reminded her. "So he contacted you. How?"

"A note was waiting for me when I got there."

"How'd you sign the register?"

"Ann Lowry." She paused. "It . . . was the name I had had all my life."

"Sure. Then how'd you get the note?"

"A man at the desk asked if anything had been left for him. When the clerk leafed through the casual mail I saw the one with Terry Massley on it."

"What did it say?"

"That today at 11 o'clock in the morning I was to walk from Eighth Avenue westward on this block and he would pick me up on the way in a cab."

"How would he recognize you?"

"He left a cheap white suitcase with a red and black college pennant pasted on either side. It was extremely conspicuous. I was to carry it on my curb side."

"I suppose it was empty."

"Of anything important . . . yes. To give it a little bulk there were a bunch of week-old newspapers in it."

"The letter," I asked, "that was straight mail?"

"Yes."

"Then how did the suitcase get there?"

"All the clerk knew was that it came by messenger. There hadn't been anything irregular about it, so he didn't remember anything special about the delivery. After I looked into the suitcase I carried out instructions. I waited until it was time, took the suitcase with me, and walked over to Eighth and started down here."

I had to turn my head so she couldn't see the look of hungry expectation in my face. The cab pick-up was another ragged edge bit that spelled hood, and I knew that some place Rhino would be waiting alive—so I could kill him. Man, it was a great feeling!

"What happened?" I asked.

"I was almost at Ninth when two men turned the corner. They walked toward me and I knew they both saw me and I saw what they wanted. I crossed the street and they did too. Then I started back and began to run. So did they. I ran in here."

"Any cabs pass at all?"

"Yes." She looked out the window, thinking back. "None stopped. He could have come by after I ran and thought I never showed up."

"He'll contact you again. Don't worry."

There was a pathetic eagerness in her voice. "You really think so?"

"I'm sure of it."

She glanced at me again, worried. "I . . . dropped the suitcase. How will . . . he know?"

"He'll find a way," I said.

I let her sit there while I showered and shaved. I found a shirt that hadn't been worn too often and put it on. There was still an unwrinkled tie and the sports jacket Vinnie insisted I hold for the fin I lent him fit as long as I didn't try to button it.

"What are you going to do?"

"I'm going to walk across town a mile or so. See some people I know. You're going to stay here, kitten. It isn't the finest, but it's the best for the moment. Leave the snaplock on, no chain, and if anybody tries to get in, duck in the closet. I don't think anybody will be back again, but just to be sure, when I get here I'll knock four times twice and you won't have to break a leg getting lost."

"All right." The nervousness faded away in a small smile. "I don't know why you're doing all this . . . but thanks, Phil."

"Forget it. It's doing me more good than it is you."

I walked to the door and she stopped me. She came over, took my hand and pressed something into it.

"Take a cab," she said.

In my palm was a twenty. It was warm and silky-feeling in my fingers and I could smell the perfume smell it had picked up from her pocketbook. I held it out to her.

"With that in my pocket I wouldn't get past the first bar. I'd drink half of it and get rolled for the rest and never get back here for three four days maybe. Here, put it back."

She made no move to take it. "That won't happen," she said softly. "Give it a try."

I didn't take a cab and I got by the first bar. But I walked across town anyway and passed a lot of bars on the way and wondered what the hell had happened to me in just a couple of hours.

When I reached Rooney's the lunch crowd had cleared out. But, as I expected, the west corner of the back room

was still noisy with half the eighth-floor staff of the great
paper up the street marking time between editions.

I slid into a booth along the wall, ordered a sandwich
and coffee, and borrowed the waiter's pad and pencil.
When he brought the lunch I handed him the note. "You
know Dan Litvak?"

His eyes indicated the back room. I handed him the
note and he walked away with it.

Dan was a tall, thin guy who seemed eternally bored
unless you could read the awareness in his eyes. He had
always moved slowly, not seeming to care what he did or
what happened to anybody. He was never a man you
could surprise with anything and when he walked up to
my booth he studied me a moment, his face expressionless, then said, "Hello, Phil," and sat down.

His eyes didn't miss a thing. With that one look he
could have read down my last 10 years in detail. I gave
him a break, though. I let him look at the twenty under
my bill so he wouldn't have to suffer the embarrassment
of thinking he was sitting through a touch.

I said, "Hello, Dan. Have some coffee?"

He waved a sign to the waiter, then sat back. "Looking for a job?"

"Hello, no. Who would hire me?"

"You don't have to go back to the same business."

"You know better than that, Dan. Anything else I'd go
nuts in."

"I know. Now let's get to the point of why you're
here."

I nodded. "Three years after I got sent up, word
reached me about Rhino Massley dying. I never bothered
finding out why or how. I want to know."

Dan toyed with the handle of his cup, turning it around
in the saucer. "The date, if you're interested, was August
10, '68. It's the kind of date you don't forget very easily.
Rhino was hit with polio in that epidemic we had that
summer. He was one of 20 some adults who had it. He
was in an iron lung up at Mayberry for a couple of
months, then the one he ordered came through and he
was shipped in it to that ranch he owns near Phoenix. He
was still handling all his business from the lung and, al-

though he wasn't going to get any better physically, he was still the rackets boss hands down."

"He died of polio?"

"No. A violent storm knocked out the power and the lung failed. The nurse on hand couldn't get the motor kicking over that ran the stand-by generator and she tried to get into town to get help. When they got back it was too late. Rhino was dead. He was buried out there."

"What happened to his estate?"

"This'll kill you. What he had, which wasn't much, only about a half million, went to polio research. Two hospitals."

"He had more than that," I said.

"Sure, but you know the mob. They're set up for that contingency. If Rhino had cash, it was ground-buried who knows where. Oh, he had plenty more, all right, and it's still wherever he put it. He couldn't take it with him after all."

Dan looked at me again, a flicker of interest in his eyes. "What's your angle?"

"You know why I got sent to the can?"

"I covered the case," Dan said flatly.

"And saw me convicted for attempting to extort money from an elected official."

"The D.A. had a good case."

"I know. The evidence was absolutely conclusive. It was black and white and open and shut. It was perhaps the most solid of any case the D.A. ever was presented with."

Dan grinned for a change. "That's right. So solid he gave it over to his newest assistant to handle who won it with ease. Your former inquisitor, by the way, is now our current D.A."

"Good for him."

His eyebrows went up. "No recriminations?"

"He wasn't in on it."

"Oh?"

"Nearly every con says he was framed."

"So I hear."

"So I was framed."

The grin came back again. "Yeah, I know."

Words didn't want to form in my mouth. I waited until my breathing was right again and I could think. "How did you know, Dan?" There was an edge on my voice.

He didn't wipe the grin off at all. "Hell, man, this is my racket, too. Nobody in our business would ever have pulled the things off they said you did. Not unless they were crazy. But now you're out and you can answer me one thing you ought to know."

"What?"

"Who did it and why?"

"Rhino, buddy. I found his protection wasn't the long green to the right people, but information he collected on them that could lay them out. I let it be known I was going after the same information and make it public and was doing pretty well when the boom came down. They sacrificed the first guy I was after, probably for a bundle paying for his chagrin of exposure, then they worked it airtight against me."

"Rough."

"That lousy sheet could have stood behind me."

"You had them on a spot."

"Nuts. They'd been on other spots before. That stinking publisher Gates . . ."

"Don't talk ill of the dead."

It was my turn to be surprised. "When?"

Dan shrugged. "A year ago. He was an editor over at Best and Hines. His heart gave out. He never did recover from losing the paper. Anyway, we're back to the first question. Why all the reminiscing?"

I looked at him across the table. "I don't think Rhino Massley is dead, friend."

He didn't say anything. He waved the waiter over, handed him my check and a buck for his back-room bill, waited until I got the change and nodded me out. We walked down the street to his office, went through the lobby to the elevators and he called off a floor.

Except for several offices and the photo lab on the north side, the picture morgue with its aisle after aisle of files took up the entire area. Dan checked at a cross file cabinet and from a big drawer brought out what he was looking for and handed it to me.

It was a four-by-four positive of Rhino Massley stretched out in a coffin ringed with bank after bank of flowers. To erase all doubt Dan handed me an eight-by-ten blowup so I could see the dead bastard in all his final glory.

When I handed it back he said, "Enough? I can get some clips from the file if you want."

I shook my head. "Don't bother."

"Why?"

"Danny boy, I'm only just starting and you don't get the short stop blues at the beginning, y'know? Photos can be faked. Rhino could have laid real still in a box for a dead shot and from here you couldn't tell the difference. Who took 'em, Dan?"

He glanced at the back of the smaller one. "Gifford," he said.

"Unimpeachable."

He rode me downstairs and walked to the street. This time I did take a cab. I got out at the corner of the block and picked up some cold cuts at the delicatessen and started toward the house. I started to say hello to Mr. Crosetti, my neighbor, then stopped and gave him my package to hold for a minute and felt my teeth all showing in a crazy kind of grin, because across the street holding down a post where they were still looking for Terry were the two hoods who had worked me over that morning.

I held my head down and the first guy didn't even bother to give me a glance. I timed the step and the swing just right and slammed my fist into his stomach just over his belt line and the immediate spasmodic folding of his body sprayed puke over everything, and when he hit the sidewalk his mouth was a wide-open hole in a frantic, twisted face.

His partner went for his gun instead of jumping me, and that was his mistake. My foot caught him in the crotch and he tried to scream and claw at his genitals and yell for help and beg for mercy all at the same time.

But I'm lousy. Real lousy. This sportsmanship crap is for TV heroes. I like it the lousy way where the hoods don't get the wrong idea about you and about coming back to get you and that kind of stuff. I kicked each one's face into a terrible bloody mess, then went back across the street, and thanked Mr. Crosetti for holding my groceries. He didn't look like he was going to be able to hold his.

I knocked four times twice and she opened the door. I stepped in quickly, closing the door with my foot, feeling suddenly breathless because she was still wet, but this time from the shower and the water droplets were like little jewels sparkling all around her, the midnight of her hair longer now, out of its soft wave and sucked tightly against her skin. The towel she held around her was too brief. Beautifully too brief. She was wider in the shoulders than I thought. Lovely round dancer's legs were a song of motion when she stepped away.

She smiled and I smiled back, then the bottom fell out of the grocery bag and when everything began to tumble she reached out instinctively and then the towel went too.

I shook my head so she'd know the groceries wouldn't matter at all and I watched while she picked up the towel, smiled once more, and walked back to the shower.

At 8 that night I got a sweater and skirt combination from Jeannie McDonald upstairs and Terry got dressed. Jeannie passed on the information that the two hoods had been picked up that afternoon by a new Buick sedan occupied by another pair of hard guys and as yet there were no repercussions.

Terry had 300 bucks in her bag and we used part of it to sign her into the Enfield Hotel just off Seventh in the Times Square area. She used the name of Ann Spencer and paid a week in advance in lieu of luggage. Luckily, she had her hotel key with her so I took it to get some of her stuff out of the Sherman. There was no doubt about her movements having been spotted and most likely the hotel was staked out, but it wasn't likely that there would be anybody on the floor.

I was right. I packed one large bag with the things she asked for and brought along the smaller over-nighter.

When I got back to the Enfield, I had her call the Sherman to ask if there were any messages for Terry Massley or Ann Lowry. The clerk said there weren't.

She put the phone down, concern deep on her face. I said, "Don't worry, he'll get in touch."

"I'm sure he will." She spun around and strode to the window.

That she sensed something was evident. She walked over and sat down opposite me. "You know my father, don't you?"

I tried to keep my face blank. "If he's the same Massley I knew once, then I do."

"What do you know about him?"

"You won't like it if I tell you."

"Perhaps not, but I'll listen."

"All right. The Massley I knew was a hood," I said. "He was the East Coast wheel for the syndicate and quite possibly head man there. He was a thief and a killer with two early falls against him, one in Chicago and one in San Francisco. A check on the back issues of any paper can verify this and, if you like, I'll be glad to supply the datelines."

She knew I wasn't lying. She said simply. "Never mind. It couldn't be the same one."

I gave her back the possibility. I said, "The Massley I knew is supposed to be dead. I've even seen pictures of him in his coffin."

"This Massley you knew," she asked, "what was his full name?"

"John Lacy Massley. He was known as Rhino."

The frown between her eyes smoothed and a smile touched her mouth. "My father was Jean Stuart Massley. So they aren't the same after all." Then the obvious finally got through to her and her hands squeezed together again. "Somebody thinks my father . . . is the . . . one you mentioned."

"Perhaps."

She held the side of her hand against her mouth and bit into her finger.

I said, "What personal effects did your mother have that might be important?"

She shook her head vacantly. "Nothing. Her marriage license, divorce papers, insurance, and bank books."

"Letters?"

"Only correspondence from the legal firm that handled the trust fund."

"Can I see all this?"

She pointed to the still unopened over-nighter. "It's all there. Do as you please."

I snapped the case open and laid the contents out on the coffee table. I went through each item, but nothing there had anything of seeming importance. All it did was make more indelible the simple fact that Terry was so sure of —I had the wrong Massley in mind.

When I turned around, I was caught in the direct stare from her eyes.

She said, "You thought my father was this other Massley, didn't you?"

I didn't try to lie out. I nodded.

"You were going to help me find him, if it had been the other one."

I nodded again, uncomfortable.

"And now that you're wrong?"

I grinned at her. She didn't waste time trying to fool you and, no matter how big and beautiful she was, she was still a dame caught alone with the shadows closing in behind her.

I said, "I'm with you, Terry. I won't bug out. You just got one hell of a slob in your corner though."

She uncurled from the chair, standing almost as tall as I was. There were lights in her eyes and when she came closer I saw they were wet. Her arms reached out and touched me, and then she was all the way there, warm and close, pressing so tightly I could feel every curve of her body melting into mine. Very softly, she said, "You're no slob," and then her mouth opened on mine and I tasted that crazy excitement again so bad I crushed her hard and tight until she threw her head back to breathe with a small, moaning sob.

I had to leave before there was more. I was finding myself with limits and inhibitions again and wondered briefly if it was going to be worth while coming back into society again. Then I knew it was and the thought passed.

Terry smiled lazily when I left and I wanted to kiss her again. But what I had in mind wouldn't make a kiss easy to take . . . or give. I was thinking louse thoughts once more. There were two J. Massleys involved and if there ever had been a name switch it would be following the common pattern to keep at least the first initial of the original name.

It only took a few minutes to locate Gifford. He was still in his office finishing off a picture series that had to be up tomorrow. He said he'd be glad to meet me for coffee in 15 minutes and named a Sixth Avenue automat for the contact.

When he arrived I called to him from a table, waited while he got his tray, then introduced myself over the coffee. Although we had never met before, I knew of his work and he remembered me.

When I told him about seeing his shots of Rhino, he screwed up his face, remembering back.

I said, "What's wrong with it?"

"Lousy shots, that's all. No class."

"You went all the way to Phoenix for them?"

Gifford shook his head. "Hell no, I was there in a private sanatorium." He tapped his chest with a thumb. "Touch of T.B. I was there four months when Rhino died."

"You ever see him around?"

"Not me. He lived on a ranch 20, maybe 30 miles off. Oh, I knew he was out there and running his business with that lung and all, but that's it."

"Then you had a good look at the body."

"Sure. It was hurried, but there he was."

I squinted and shook my head impatiently. "Like how? Tell me."

"What's to tell? I got a call from the paper at the time to get a body shot of Rhino for the night edition. At the time it was pretty big news and I was at the spot, so it wasn't unreasonable to ask. I went over the day they were having the funeral, managed to get by the professional criers and found this woman who was in charge of things. She didn't like it, but she let me into the room where the casket was for a quick shot."

"Who was this woman, family?"

"No, Rhino left no family except for some cousins who weren't there. She had been his nurse as I remember. Quite a looker."

"Then who were the mourners?"

"Hell, you can imagine. Hoods, politicians who wanted to stay in with the next-in-line, whoever it would be, the usual business. You know."

"Sure."

Gifford studied me. "Anything special in this? Like with pictures?"

"I don't know. I'm groping. Tell me, what did the body look like?"

He made a gesture with his shoulders. "What do they all look like? Dead. Waxy. Only difference here was the coffin wasn't the kind that opened down to the waist. Rhino's body was so twisted they kept him covered to the neck. All you could see was his face and the tips of his fingers where they crossed on his chest." He paused, fingered his mouth thoughtfully, then added, "As I remember, they only opened the casket for a short time so the public could have one last, quick look. Rhino had been pretty sensitive about his condition and had left orders to that effect."

"He was buried there?"

"Yup. Cemetery out near the hills. They didn't keep him around long, either. He was planted two days after he died."

"Oh?"

Gifford drummed on the table top with his fingers. "How come all the interest?"

"I had the idea Rhino Massley could still be alive."

For a moment his face took on a thoughtful look, then he shook his head. "I've seen dead men before."

"Anybody in a coffin automatically looks dead," I told him.

"Good assumption. Go on."

"Some makeup, total immobilization, easy to achieve in a three-quarters' casket, only allow a quick, unstudied look, and live men can seem pretty damn dead."

"Reasonable, but that's assuming something else."

"What?"

"His motive."

And that was that. There wasn't any damn motive in the world. He was already on top, he had no place to go that an iron lung couldn't be spotted, and no reason to fake his death anyway.

I thanked Gifford and broke up the party.

I turned south on Sixth, walking aimlessly back to the Enfield. Overhead a low rumble shook the night and I could smell the rain in the air. It started before I reached the end of the block and it felt good. Anything was better than that down-the-drain feeling of knowing your grand hopes had been washed right out of existence.

Damn that Rhino anyway, why the hell couldn't he have stayed alive! I would have choked him as he lay in that lung of his and laughed in his face when he died. I would have given anything to have been there the night the power blew out. Man, I could have watched him die by inches in his cell like I did in mine. I could have watched his face in that mirror over his head beg for me to do something and, while he kicked off inch by inch, I could have toasted his passing with a cold brew.

I stood there on the corner waiting for the light to change, and then just as suddenly as it had turned sour it turned sweet again. In a way it was reaching for straws, but it made me feel good and light-headed like before when there was a purpose left in life yet, and this started with an assumption too.

Assuming that Terry's father *was* Rhino Massley, then somehow he *did* have a reason for playing dead.

And with that the big second assumption was laid right out in front of me. If Rhino was alive, then he had not only been assumed dead, but assumed sick too. No polio victim in a lung could hide out long anywhere, far less travel around!

I grinned at the night and held my face up to the rain. I was going against all logic and flying in the face of the classic objectiveness we had been taught to observe. It was a crazy Don Quixote move, only on the other end there might possibly be a real giant.

I opened the door of my flat and switched on the light. The two boys sitting together on the couch and pointing the cold round noses of the automatics at me stood up. They were different ones, these. Neither smiled.

The taller one said, "Turn around and let's go."

"Where?"

"You talk too much," he told me. His hand gave an easy push, a hint, but it was enough. I turned around and headed outside again. The car was there at the curb, the back door open. I got in with one on either side.

In a way it was funny. Ten years of being alone, hating every minute of it. Now when I wanted it, what did I get . . . togetherness. I started to laugh and the hood on my right looked at me like I had spilled a few marbles.

On the East Side there's a steak house known as Ruby's and from the back room, across a platterful of T-bone, Mannie Waller did his business. His side was a private little niche with a phone, a walnut humidor of cigars and a shelf of light wine that was all he would drink. He was a big heavy pig of a guy who ate himself into obesity but in doing it kept out of the line of fire and inherited a fat hunk of the underworld business when the others knocked themselves off.

Nobody knew just where Mannie stood, but nobody was trying to push him out, either. Talk had it that Mannie was a Syndicate man, a paymaster for the uptown boys. He was part of a new quiet mob that had moved in and taken over after the Appalachin fiasco.

And now Mannie was looking up at me, wiping the grease from his chin. He said, "Sit down."

I took too long. The hood beside me gave me a cut in the gut with the edge of his hand and I folded into the chair.

Mannie said, "No hands, Joe. You know what he did to Jolly and Hal."

"That why you dragged me down here?"

He hunched his fat shoulders and grinned again. "Not entirely, but still I got to keep telling you little guys. One gets tough, the others try it, and then I got trouble. We like to keep things quiet. The boys were only doing a job." He belched and settled back in his chair. "They look for a girl. She ran in your place. You know something about this?"

"You know what I know. Them idiots bust in and looked around. They know what they saw."

"Sure. Nothing. They look all through that tenement

and find the same thing. Only trouble is she don't get out on the roof or through the cellar and she don't have time to get any place else but to your joint."

"So?"

"So she knows where she's going."

"You're nuts."

Joe's gun muzzle slashed the top of my head open. It turned my skull into a white hot sheet of flame that took too long to subside. Mannie was nodding approvingly, waiting.

Mannie said, "Maybe I'm wrong. Me, I got to be sure. You know where this dame is, you tell me. I got a C waiting. You want to hold out . . . so it's your funeral. Maybe later we find out we're wrong and you got to take a beating for no reason. I send you a C anyway. I'm a good guy. Meantime, you gotta hurt a little. You know how it is."

"Yeah," I said, "I know how it is, but since when are you playing it stupid?"

His brows twitched and rose in a slow gesture of surprise. "You think I am that, eh?"

"You're sure showing all the signs. What would anybody want with me?"

Mannie enjoyed his moment. He scraped his chair back from the table, folded his hands over his stomach, and smiled. "Now, that is something to think about, hey? So I'll tell you." He licked his lips with contentment and rumbled a laugh like Sidney Greenstreet used to in the Humphrey Bogart movies.

"The girl she runs in and don't come out. She don't have time to go anywhere but your place. Now, if you're a nothing, then she comes out. But if you're a something, then maybe not. So we ask around about you and find out some funny things. Used to be a big shot, hey? Reporter, and a hot one. You laid out Anthony Smith's bunch after the war and you was the guy who went to town on the Petersen snatch. You sure was a big one until you held out the wrong hand."

"So what?"

"So you're big two ways. This girl, when she runs she goes straight to the only big brain around who at the same time is muscle enough to take care of things the hard way. In all the block there's nobody but bums and punks and hookers. You're the only big one . . ." he pointed a finger at me to make his point ". . . and to you she goes."

"Look . . ."

"No," Mannie said. "You talk to me and I listen, but I won't look. Where is the girl?"

I spit on the floor in front of his feet. "Drop dead," I told him.

Mannie smiled indulgently again, his thick lips wetly red like fresh opened meat. "Take him upstairs, Joe," he said.

The rod went in my ribs again, a cold round rudder that showed me the way to the back, the iron staircase going to the third floor, the steel fire door, and the big room inside. It steered me toward the wall where the packing cases were and sensed when I was going to make my move because it beat me to the trick with a quick downward slash and I was all sobbing pain again, trying to yell out against the fire in my head and the insistent drumming of heavy feet on my ribs.

There were times when they would stop and ask about the girl and twice I almost told them but they didn't let me get my breath and after that I couldn't tell them. Then the feet and the hands and even the things they used stopped hurting and started to be nothing more than a nuisance and far-away sounds, and I drifted off into the deep black that's at the end of time.

They had used wire on my wrists and ankles and just left me there on the floor. I stared at the bare wood, tasted the dirt that had been ground into my mouth, and saw the dark red of the splotches my blood had made.

Any movement was pure torture and, when I managed to turn over, my breathing became a series of convulsive sobs that tried to tear my chest out. Somehow I got on my knees, my hands behind my back, fighting the terrible cramps that racked at pounded and beaten muscle tissue.

To one side, the heavily-barred window was showing a brighter gray now. Somewhere beyond the apartments and office buildings the sun was rising and soon the city would too.

There wasn't much time left.

Near me was a spool of baling wire. The two lengths I had been wrapped in came from that reel and seeing it there burned a little hole in my brain until I realized what it meant. There had to be cutters around somewhere.

I had to roll over completely three times to reach the packing crate. I lay on my side and lashed out with my feet until I had the crate rocking and finally tilted up against the wall. The next kick brought it over and with it the cutters that had been lying on top.

It was almost impossible to force life into my hands, but somehow it happened. I knelt there, fingering the cutters, and finally cut through the strands around my legs. It made life more bearable for a while and made it easier to recover the tool when I dropped it trying to free my hands.

Then it was done and the sun was a bright thing laying a wide band of light across the floor while it brought to life the city outside. There was a toilet and a basin in a cubicle in the corner and I soaked myself down, washing the cuts and cleaning the grime and dried blood from my face. It was bad, but I had awakened other times when it had been just as bad.

The band of sunlight was touching the far wall when I heard them coming. They stopped several times because Mannie Waller couldn't make the stairs all at once. Near the top, one got impatient as I knew he would and came on ahead. I laid the hunk of piping I had picked up across his head and caught him before he fell. I had him out of the way and his .38 in my hand before the other came in. The other one tried to yell before the pipe came down but it never reached his lips. The pipe smashed his forehead into a bloody mess and he tumbled into my arms and slid to the floor.

When Mannie came in the white sickness showed on his face and he stood still, absolutely still, trying hard to take his eyes off the two on the floor. He knew I had to be behind him. He knew I'd have a rod and he knew he was real close to being dead.

Touching the back of his skull with the muzzle of the .38 was only a gesture, but the effect was beautiful. Big Mannie, the Boss, the Head Man, went into a violent fit of trembling, making whimpering sounds that had a pleading tone to them.

I used the wire on all of them, twisted hard into the flesh so that you could barely see it. When Joe moaned and opened his eyes I kicked him insensible and let Mannie see it. Then I squatted down beside the fat man, the clippers in my hand opening and shutting suggestively, and in that movement and metallic sound he read all the terrible things that could possibly happen to him and his eyes rolled in his head.

I said, "You're going to talk, Mannie. I heard some things so I know what's going on, and if you lie I'll know it and it will be the last lie you'll tell me. You understand?"

He couldn't talk. Spit ran out of his mouth as he bobbed his head, never taking his eyes from the clippers.

"Who is the girl?"

Mannie wet his lips, trying desperately to say something. He finally made it. "Massley's kid."

"Rhino's?"

His jowls shook again with the nod. "Yeah, Rhino."

I paused, savoring the next moment. "He's alive then?"

The expression on his face made me wish I hadn't asked it. Even in his fear he was completely puzzled by it. He shook his head, swallowed hard, and said, "Rhino . . . he's dead."

"Then why do you want the girl?"

He tried not to say it, but when I moved those clippers toward his mouth he couldn't keep it in at all. "Rhino left papers . . . his wife had them."

"What kind of papers?"

"Big papers. They could send up lots of guys. They were . . . Rhino's cover . . . his protection. He even could break up . . . the organization with them."

"Why didn't you get them before this?"

"His woman. She knew where he kept them but she disappeared. Nobody knows until she dies where she is."

"What about the girl?"

"So she gets the papers, don't she? She comes east, what for if not to make contacts and use them. She's big trouble to everybody. She will die."

"And you were elected to kill her?"

He blubbered softly until I touched him with the clippers again. "I get orders . . . you know," he whimpered.

"From who?"

His eyes tried to bug out and his tongue was even too dry to dampen his mouth. "How . . . can I know. It's by phone. I get the word . . . then I do it."

"Names, Mannie."

You could smell the fear coming from his pores. He tried to talk and couldn't. "Okay," I said with a fat grin, "so maybe you don't know, but let me put in a word, too. If she dies, so will you, fatty."

"No! No . . . anybody will kill this girl. She is dangerous to many big people."

"But if she dies, you'll be right behind her, understand?"

He knew I wasn't going to kill him then. He nodded quickly, eager to please, then I gave him a boot that wiped all the eagerness off. I did it enough, so he knew what it was like to play it like back in the old days, and walked out. Only they wouldn't have it so easy. I still had the clippers in my back pocket.

I took another cab and waited until I got back to my place again before I let it all come through to me, bit by bit. I cleaned up right, shaved, and spoke to myself in the mirror. All the bits and pieces were starting to pull together and show signs of belonging to an orderly whole.

It made a nice, satisfying picture with only one ugly blot in the middle. Perhaps Rhino wasn't alive, but Terry still came from his loins. It was going to be hard to tell her that. But at the moment the prime thing was to keep her hidden. She was the target in the game from every angle. Orders were for the mob to take her. On top of that somebody else was dealing himself into the game. Somebody who said he was her father.

At the corner I called Dan Litvak and asked him to meet me in Rosario's in an hour. He got there right after

I did, raised his eyebrows a little when he saw my face, but made no comment at all.

I said, "I need another favor, Dan. Check through the files and run down a Jean Stuart Massley."

"Still on that kick?"

"It's looking up."

"Anything you can tell me?"

I brought him up to date with all the details. His face never changed, but in back of his eyes strange things were happening. He let me finish, then said, "You think both Massleys were the same?"

"Could be."

"And if Rhino Massley is, as he seems to be . . . dead?"

I shrugged, "Then I want his papers. This whole thing started over those documents. I lost seven years because of them and now I want some kicks."

"Have you tried being sensible about the bit?"

"Like how?"

"Like how, if you handle this right, you can throw it back in a lot of faces the right way and maybe get back on top again. Make a story of it and every sheet in the country will want you on the staff."

"Nuts."

"Think it over anyway." He swilled the coffee down and climbed out of the booth. "Anything else you want?"

"Yes. Find out who the doctor was who handled Rhino's case. If you can get his medical history, so much the better."

"That shouldn't be hard."

I called from the Enfield Hotel lobby and she sounded a little breathless. It was as if she had been expecting me and all the anticipation showed in a few husky words. It was a heady feeling, thinking there was someone waiting. It had been a long time since there had been anything like that. And now it was only a thought and a foolish one at that. Who the hell was I to invite such thoughts at all? Phil Rocca, ex-con, the big nothing. Sweaty underwear, dirty shirt and somebody else's coat. Great.

Upstairs was a lovely woman. She was waiting, all right, because I might have some news about her old man. When I told her what I had, she wouldn't be waiting any more. *So forget it, idiot boy. Let her just be something that happened and nothing more. Let's not get hurt again.*

But it didn't happen like that. She was a smiling Valkyrie standing in the doorway, hair like a black waterfall on her shoulders and her hands out to take mine. Her eyes were laughing and her mouth told me she missed me. She laid her cheek against mine and squeezed my arm, then suddenly realized that there was a difference and her eyes went wide and she traced the shoe marks on my face with the tips of her fingers.

She asked, "Again?" and when I nodded she dropped her face into her hand and remained that way until I tilted her chin up.

"They were the same persons?"

"No, but the same outfit."

"What . . . did they want?"

I told her a half truth. "To teach me a lesson. They didn't like me roughing up the hoods who started this party rolling."

She studied me, then said, "It's my father, isn't it?"

"I'm not sure yet."

"When will you be sure?"

"Soon."

There wasn't long to wait. The phone rang sharply twice and when I picked it up Dan said, "Phil?"

"Here, Dan."

"I have that dope you wanted.

"Jean Stuart Massley was Rhino's real name, but the guy had a phobia about effeminate names and changed it some place along the line. Apparently he hated women and this is what led to his divorce. His early record includes assault raps, mainly brought by women. He wouldn't even employ a female secretary. So he changed his name. Jean Stuart was pretty frilly to him. The John Lacy tag he used was the name of a fighter back in the old days, so he went along with that."

"Got the other?"

"Sure. The doctor was Thomas Hoyt. If you remember, he was the one the mob used back during the war. He was an alcoholic, but they straightened him out and put him back in business."

"Where is he?"

"Still in Phoenix, I imagine. He's not licensed in New York any longer. I couldn't pick up that medical history. It went with Hoyt from Mayberry to Phoenix and is probably still there. One of the old dames at Mayberry said it was a pretty quiet affair all the way around. Hoyt brought in a nurse from outside and nobody was allowed near Rhino at all while he was there. She supposed they were afraid of someone coming in and knocking Rhino off and it's a pretty good guess."

"Who was the nurse?"

"I didn't ask. Want me to check?"

"Never mind."

I hung up the phone and turned around. Terry hadn't moved.

"Now you know," she said.

"That's right. Now I know."

"You'll tell me?"

I nodded. "Rhino Massley was your father."

A shadow crossed her face. "You said he was dead."

"I said I thought he was dead. It's beginning to look like there isn't any other answer."

"But you're not sure."

"I will be."

"If he *is* dead, then, who is pretending to be my father?"

There wasn't any other way except to spell it out. I said, "Your father was a hood. He had documentary evidence that kept the right people in line and used it to stay on top. Your mother either lifted that stuff from him or he gave it to her to hold."

"But she never . . ."

"He might have had that much contact with her. She could still be useful even if she was divorced. Don't forget that Rhino was a louse." Her mouth pulled tight. "Sorry, kid, but that's the way it was."

"I understand."

"When it came out who your mother was, the mob assumed those documents would come to light, most likely in the inheritor's hands, which was you. They slapped a tail on you, not willing to move in until they knew where you were keeping the stuff.

"Then when they got wind of somebody else trying to con in on the deal they had to scratch off fast. They couldn't take a chance on anyone else getting it. If they could pick you up, they could squeeze out the information. If necessary, you were expendable. Knock you off and they could have time to search out what they wanted."

"But Phil . . ."

"What?"

"There isn't anything. You saw what mother left." Her eyebrows drew together in a puzzled frown. "There never has been anything. Surely she would have told me if there had been."

"Perhaps not. I want to look at that stuff again."

"Go ahead. I haven't touched it."

This time I dumped the lot on the bed and spread it out. I went over the papers searching for answers, but there was no more now than there had been.

To myself I said, "There has to be something else."

Terry heard me, came over and stood beside me and reached into her pocket-book. She handed me a leather folder. "Mother's wallet. She never carried a purse."

I took it from her fingers, opened the snap and leafed through the plastic card holders inside. There was her driver's license, membership cards in local clubs, several gas credit cards, and two from L.A. restaurants. One folder held several news clippings, brittle and yellow, reporting events Terry had participated in in school. There were photos of her as a girl, two winter clothes storage receipts, a season ticket for the L.A. Dodger games, and a dime-thin ten-dollar gold piece.

"Did it help?"

"I can't see how," I told her. I put everything back where it was and handed it to her.

"Phil . . ."

Without realizing it, I had my arms around her, only now it was as if we had known each other a long, long time and I wasn't what I was at all. Her hair had the fragrance of some wild flower that I could pick whenever I wanted to. She lifted her head, her eyes going over my face. I kissed her gently, her eyes closing when our mouths touched. It was only for a moment, then I held her close and wondered where all the crazy hate went that I felt when I first saw her. And how long ago was it to then . . . years?

She said, "What shall I do?"

"What do you want to do?"

"If I stay somebody might . . . be hurt. It . . . might be you, Phil."

"I'm nobody. It wouldn't matter at all."

"To me it would."

My fingers tightened on her arms and she winced, but didn't try to pull away. "Don't talk like that. We haven't anything in common at all."

For a moment her face was blank, then shame and sudden shock touched her as with a strange hand, and the wetness that welled into her eyes overflowed to her cheeks and I could feel the sob working in her chest.

"Because my father . . . was this man . . . I'm no good. That's why, isn't it?"

Amazement pulled my face tight. "Are you crazy?" I said. "Sugar, I don't give a fat damn what your father was. You're class, kitten. You're a big, lovely woman with more class than a guy hardly ever gets to see at all."

"Phil . . ."

"No, just listen. I'm a bum, a slob. I did time, even if it was a bad rap, and things like that change a guy and stick with him a long while. All I had in my head in the beginning was to get the chance to knock off your old man and that one hope kept me going. For a while I thought I had it again. I was all geared up to kill and no matter what it cost I was ready for it. Knocking Rhino over would have been the happiest day of my life.

"Not now. You spoiled the picture for me. I could still hate him with everything inside me, but because you wanted him I couldn't touch him. That's what you've done to me. You got me all crazy gone and I can't even look at you without wanting to put my hands on you and I'm thinking all kinds of things I thought I had forgotten.

"But I'm not letting it rub off on you, girl. One touch of me and you'd be dirtied too, and the best thing I can do is to go back where I belong and let you alone. I'm going to run this bit down. I'm going to get it straight so nobody will be holding a sword over your head ever, and when I do it it's going to be so-long all the way and that's that."

Her hair shimmered with motion when she shook her head. "You can't do that, Phil."

"The hell I can't. Maybe another time it would have been different, but this is here and now and that's how it's going to be. Look at me. I'm lousy and dirty and a couple of days ago I was scrubbing for handouts so I could buy a jug. I run with the sewer rats now because there's no place else to go. I don't even care any more, can't you tell? I like it this way. I can sit back and spit on the world and there's not a thing it can take away from me because I haven't got anything. So take a good look, kid, and you can see why I don't want anything rubbing off."

The tears were still there in eyes that were large and dark. "I don't see all those things at all," she said simply.

I took her hands away and held them. "You're all mixed up. So I did you a favor. I'll do one more. Keep it that way. Just say thanks and let it go."

She smiled, wiped back the tears that stained her cheeks, and said, *"You're* mixed up. If you think I'm going to let go of you just when I found you, then you're *really* mixed up."

Her hand came up and lightly stroked the side of my face. "There isn't any more past for either one of us. There is only now and later. Alone neither of us will be anything. Together we can be much. I want you, Phil."

This time I didn't try to keep her off.

Softly, she said, "Phil . . . I love you."

There wasn't any need to answer her. She knew. . . .

The Mayberry Sanatorium was a private institution 30 miles outside the city. It was a two-story, brick building set in the center of 15 acres and had been the private retreat of the wealthy for the past half century.

I had been up there a few times interviewing patients for the paper, and as far as I knew it had an excellent reputation. The head nurse was a Miss Mulligan, a good

60 years a spinster lady, but quick as a roach on her feet and with eyes that could snap the tail off a cat across a stone stoop.

For a moment I thought she remembered me, but the curiosity in her face passed and she acknowledged our introduction with a nod. I said, "A Mr. Litvak called here earlier for some information on a former patient."

"That's right. A police matter about Massley. That was some time ago."

"You gave him the information."

"I did."

"I see. Perhaps you can add a few points. Mr. Litvak said that the case had been handled very quietly."

"Secretly would be more like it."

"Did you see the patient?"

"Several times."

"He was . . . sick?"

This time her eyebrows shot up, then she saw what I meant. "We do get patients doing nothing more than recovering from prolonged drunkenness, or merely escaping from an unattractive home life or unpleasant business, but Mr. Massley certainly wasn't like that."

"Why not?"

"If you're going to feign sickness, there are easier and less expensive ways than faking polio."

"Uh-huh. Could be. Did you see him out of the lung?"

"Yes. I passed by when he was being handled. He was able to stay out a maximum of 30 minutes. However, neither I nor any staff nurse handled him. He had his own nurse."

"Who was she, do you remember?"

She rose, went to a wall cabinet, and opened the top drawer. From it she drew a folder, checked it, then handed it to me. "Everything is here."

The name at the top was Elena Harris. The hospital form she had filled out listed her age as 32, her address in the East 70s, and stated that she had graduated from a southern university and served at six different hospitals since. A letter of recommendation was included, written on Dr. Hoyt's stationery. At the bottom was a 2 × 2 photo of Nurse Harris that was typical of identification photographs in all respects except one. No camera and no uniform could make her anything else than beautiful.

"Pretty," I said.

"That was her trouble." There was no malice in her statement, merely indifference.

I tapped the photo. "She seems familiar."

"Possibly. She was a type."

"Like how?"

"One to turn men's heads. She was a distracting influence while she was here."

"That was her trouble you mentioned?"

Miss Mulligan's nod was curt, again without any seeming malice. "She caused . . . well, rivalries, especially among the younger doctors."

"Deliberately?"

"No, I wouldn't say it was deliberate."

"Was she efficient?"

"I found no cause for complaint. Certainly Mr. Massley was satisfied. She scarcely ever left him. In fact, she was more than nurse to him."

"Oh?" I looked at her and waited.

"She took care of all his correspondence and seemed to be the intermediary between him and his business contacts. There were times when she acted rather the secretary than the nurse."

"You checked on her, of course."

"Naturally. In fact, she had an excellent scholastic record. As you notice, however, Mr. Massley was her first case in four years, although that isn't anything unusual. Quite often one returns to practice for private patients."

"I see. Can I keep this picture?"

"Yes. We have a duplicate upstairs."

"Thanks. Now, if it's within the realm of professional ethics, you might add something."

"We'll see."

"What is your personal opinion of Miss Harris?"

At first I thought she would ignore the question entirely, then she said, "Could you give me a practical reason for your inquiry?"

Her eyes had seen a little too much of the world to be fooled by a lie or taken in by half truths.

I said, "Massley was a hood. When he died he left behind information dangerous to certain persons. They think Massley's daughter has his documents and she's in line to be killed unless I can find them first. It's possible that anyone who was close to Massley could come up with something." I paused for a deep breath. "Now, what about her?"

Miss Mulligan's mouth tightened into a thin line, her nostrils pinched tight above it. "I see. Then perhaps my opinion won't be unethical. I mentioned that Harris was first, a nurse. Secondly, she was a confidante of a sort. Third, in her personal relationship with Mr. Massley I had the impression that he had been, or was, her lover."

"How did you determine that?"

For the first time Miss Mulligan showed the dull flush of emotion kept well under control. Her blush was faint, but definite. Her eyes left mine and sought her desk top.

"Our rooms do not have locks on the doors," she said a little breathlessly.

"I see. Were they aware that you happened on their . . . intimacies?"

A gentle whisper of a shudder touched Mulligan's shoulders and with a far away gesture her tongue touched her lips, almost wistfully. "No," she said hesitantly. "They were . . . engrossed."

"But the lung . . . ?"

"What they . . . the lung didn't . . ." Then the deep red flooded up from her starched collar and she turned away quickly.

I let it stay there. Whatever could bring a flush to her face needed little further explanation.

I thanked her, but I don't think she heard me. I slipped the picture of Elena Harris in my jacket pocket, picked up my hat, and left. There was still a half hour before train time back into Manhattan, so I wasted it over coffee at the station diner.

From Grand Central I called Terry and had her meet me for supper at Lum Fong's. The junior executive crowd was there at the bar as usual, the deliberately casual eyes that scanned us via the big mirror showing almost professional consternation because they couldn't figure how a guy like me had a dame like her.

"You're lovely, doll," I told her. "Everybody here has eyes for you."

"You like it that way?"

She smiled, but now it was to hide the concern that came back again. "Is the trouble still big?"

"It's big." I told her most of the details of my visit with Miss Mulligan, then. "It could get bigger. Look, how much money can you get hold of fast?"

"I have $1,500 in traveler's checks at the hotel. Why?"

"I want to go to Phoenix. Phoenix is where your father . . . supposedly died. There may be some answers there. Now, do I get financed?"

"On one condition."

I raised my eyebrows and waited.

"That I go along," she said.

"Forget it. This won't be a fun trip and I can travel faster alone. Besides, I have something for you to do."

"Like what?"

I took Elena Harris' photo out of my pocket and handed it to her. "It's a little thought I have," I said. "Beautiful women usually make a stab at show business some time or another. In the process they leave their pictures around. Do you think you could comb the agencies who might know something? I could . . ."

She didn't let me finish. She grinned and said, "I know the ropes. All of them. Many was the time I made the rounds. But can't I do this and go with you too?"

"No, because I want you to stick around to see about that contact at the Sherman."

The sudden stricken look of an animal caught off guard touched her face with fine taut lines. She was remembering the happy thought she had had in the beginning, the thought of seeing her father, and now, once again, she was being reminded that she never really had one.

"Is it . . . really necessary now?"

"Somehow that contact is a key to all this. It has to be run down."

"Phil . . ."

"Whoever it was is dangerous. The stakes are high in

this game and you make up the rules as you go along. You're a necessary factor in the game because, as far as anybody is concerned, you know old Rhino's secret. Keep them in the dark and we'll have the edge."

"But we can't fight those people, Phil."

"I don't intend to," I said. "I know when to holler for the troops."

"Like when?"

"Like now."

I went to the row of phone booths at the back of the room and put in a call for Dan. When he answered I said, "Dan, I want to see the D.A. tonight. Can you arrange it?"

There was the queer sound of silence a second, then incredulously Dan said, "Cal Porter?"

I could almost see him shrug. "I'll see what I can do. Give me five minutes."

I let him have the time. When I called back he had the information. "Porter is at his desk right now having been called away from a supper party to preside at the questioning of a hot suspect in last night's park kill. He said he'd see you."

When I came back I hurried Terry into a cab and up to the hotel. She cashed $500 in traveler's checks, gave me the bundle, a smile, and a kiss for good luck.

"Be careful, Phil. Please."

"Don't worry about me. You're the one on the spot. I'm an idiot for letting you stand alone, but there isn't anybody else. If you get in trouble, you call Dan Litvak or the cops. Don't stop to think it out . . . just call."

"I will. You'll be back soon?"

"Two days will do it."

She smiled, her mouth softly damp, coming closer to mine. "I'll miss you," she said.

Dan's call opened the door for me, not too widely, but enough for five minutes of the big man's time. Cal Porter had turned gray over the years, the leanness of youth lost to the thickening effect of middle age.

He stood up when I entered and said, "Mr. Rocca?" It was merely a formal question.

I nodded.

"Sit down, please." He turned briefly and smiled at the hawk-faced woman clutching the steno pad. "You needn't stay, Miss Marie. We'll finish in the morning."

Porter didn't waste any time. "Dan Litvak said you have something on your mind."

"I need some information, Mr. Porter."

He reached for a cigarette and lit it without taking his eyes off mine. "Why?"

"Because it might help me bust a story, that's why."

"This has something to do with you personally." Again it was a statement.

"I wouldn't give a damn, otherwise," I told him. "I wasn't exactly rehabilitated in the can, Mr. Porter. I came out with about as much regard for the human race as I have for malaria and, if I had my choice between the two, I'd have taken the disease."

Porter let a small, grim smile touch his mouth. "That sounds like a former attitude. What is it now?"

"I haven't decided yet. I'm walking the fence."

"Any preference which way you want to jump?"

I shrugged. "I could be influenced."

"All right," he said unexpectedly, "how can I help?"

Before I could speak he took a deep pull on the butt, poked it out in an ash tray, and leaned back in his chair. "I'll tell you why I'm interested, Rocca. You may not realize it, but I made my reputation prosecuting your case. Secondly, knowing of your past abilities, I'm quite willing to make use of anything you might have to take another step."

"Like over my dead body?"

"That's right. If it will take me closer to the tall chair in Albany."

"Now you want to be governor," I said. I could feel my face start to tighten. "You're awfully friendly, Mr. Porter. I'm a punk, remember? Seven years con time and now a barnacle in tenement row and not a nickel's worth of whiskey credit."

"I've kept track." he told me. "Besides, Litvak is no fool. He thinks you're up to something. Now what do you want to know?"

Without sparring around I said, "When Rhino Massley died, what was the condition of the mobs?"

His expression changed slowly, not so much in his face as in the squint of his eyes and a tightening of his shoulders. He leaned forward on the desk, lacing his fingers together.

"You can read the papers."

"Nuts, buddy. You have more than that. It would have come out except that his kicking off left you holding a half-filled bag."

He waited a moment, then: "Very well. The mobs, let's say, were in good condition. Their activities increased ten times while law enforcement agencies remained at the same level. Crime of every sort has been on the increase about 15 per cent or better each year. When Massley died it was, like now, at a peak. The cost of living index has gone up on all fronts, you see."

"Good. Now did Massley's death put any kind of a dent in mob activities?"

His fingers were showing white now and there were taut lines around his mouth. For a moment I thought he would hedge, then he looked at me seriously. "At the time nobody was willing to admit that there was such a thing as a Syndicate. The Mafia was active, but under control, and organized gangs seemed to have only local prominence.

"However, we found out later that in the face of increased activity on the part of such gangs, a close liaison was necessary for obvious business reasons. A large scale pseudo-legitimate setup was necessary to front for criminal deals and an underworld bank sort of thing required to have ready funds for any new enterprise.

"Massley, we believe, was the banker. When he died there was quite a bit of consternation in various quarters and certain phases of action we had been alerted against failed to come off. The conclusion was that the money wasn't available for it."

"What happened to it?"

Porter shrugged. "Frankly, we don't know."

"Can you guess?"

The frown came back again. "I can," he said. He paused, unlaced his fingers, and folded his arms across his chest. "The 'bank' wasn't really big yet . . . it was in the trial stage, so to speak. My guess is that whoever took over after Massley had access to the money."

I shook my head. "You're playing games with me now. You want me to try?"

Porter nodded and sat there waiting. I said, "That was hidden money. Massley alone knew where it was. He didn't expect to die, so he wasn't setting himself up as a target for some outside operator to shoot at by making its whereabouts common knowledge or even putting it on paper. Massley was right at his job when he died and that loot is still around." I grinned at him. "How's that one?"

Porter's face had a courtroom look now. "And you know where it is?"

"No."

"You think you might have a lead?"

"Maybe. To even bigger things."

"Explain."

This time I laughed at him. "No, not now, buddy. I have some pretty wild ideas that I'm going to make pay off one way or another. If I'm right and you go along, they can even get you that tall chair in Albany. If I'm wrong nobody gets hurt but me."

"I see."

"I don't think you do, but thanks for talking to me. It was good to see you again after all these years."

He scowled but didn't say anything. I stood up and put on my hat. "There's one more thing I'd like you to know, Mr. Porter. It doesn't make any difference any more, but I'd just like to get things straight."

"Oh?"

I grinned at his expression. "The rap you got your reputation on was a bum one, buddy. Massley had me framed like a Van Gogh original and you went the route to make it stick. That's water over the falls now and I just don't give a damn about it any more. But it's just something I'd like you to keep in mind, okay?"

He knew then. He knew it as well as I knew it, but with him it came too quickly and the thought of it was a little too big to swallow all at once. His face got a pasty white color that was a wordless apology and a soundless attempt at explaining away the naïveté that comes with boundless ambition in public service.

I grinned again and left his office. Things were looking up again. One of his news items, properly placed in the scheme of things, pointed to an answer. That is, if certain other items fell properly into place.

I didn't bother with any baggage. I had been a slob too long to let a change of drawers bother me when I was in a hurry. I grabbed the bus out to Kennedy and picked up a ticket at the desk. I needn't have hurried because no flight was leaving until 7:50 and that gave me three hours to wait.

Two newspapers and a magazine later I still had an hour to kill and wandered to the men's room. That took care of 15 minutes. I unlocked the door to my dime booth, took one step out and thought, in the tiny second I could still think, that my brains went all over the room.

That took care of another 30 minutes. I was able to convince the two cops that I fell, but the doctor wasn't buying it. He said nothing, but I knew what he was thinking. The cops were all for throwing me out until I produced my ticket, then they helped me to a bench outside where I could wait until plane time.

The 30 bucks I had loose in my side pocket were gone. The rest of the bundle was safe way back under my shirt and for once it paid to have a few bindle stiff habits. I cursed silently at the pain in my skull and wondered what kind of an artist was shrewd enough to spot dough riding with a seedy looking character like me.

When the flight was announced, I got on, took two of the pills the doctor gave me, and didn't wake up until we hit Phoenix.

It was hot in Phoenix. I took a taxi to town, had a large bowl of chili at the counter in the bus terminal, then found the address of the Board of Health in the phone directory.

The girl at the desk was a lovely tanned kid, in an off-the-shoulder Mexican blouse, with a quick smile, who said hello in a breathless way that made me wonder what she was doing working for the city. She took one look at my clothes and said, "Visitor?"

I said, "I'm trying to find a doctor."

"You don't look sick." Her mouth hid a smile.

"What I got a doctor won't cure, sugar." She blushed a little and made a face at me. "The doctor I want is a Thomas Hoyt. He was out here several years ago."

"Hoyt." She put a knuckle to her teeth, thought a moment, then said, "I know who you mean. Let me find out." It didn't take long. She came back with two cards she had scribbled notations on. She glanced at me, then asked, "Friend?"

"No."

She seemed relieved somehow. "Oh. Well . . . Dr. Hoyt is dead. He's been dead quite a few years."

"What happened?"

"I really don't know, but he died. October second, 1965."

The cold feeling hit me again. Inside, everything seems to drop out momentarily and it never does go back into place right. "You're sure? There wouldn't be two Dr. Hoyts?"

She shook her head. "I'm positive."

Outside I had the cabby take me down to the newspaper offices and I paid him off there.

Everybody was friendly in Phoenix. They all smiled and were all glad to help. The young fellow I asked about seeing back issues of the sheet took personal charge and brought back the issue I wanted. I sat down at a table, spread out the paper, and found the story about Dr. Thomas Hoyt on an inside page.

It was all very simple, very cut and dried. He and a friend by the name of Leo Grant were coming back from a hunting trip in the mountains, tried to take a turn too fast in their jeep, and hurtled off the road. Both were killed and it was several days before the wreck or the bodies were found.

I just started on the interesting part when the tall fellow in a short-sleeved sport shirt sat down beside me and said, "Howdy."

I said hello as politely as I could.

"My name is Stack. Joe Stack," he told me. "I handle police stuff."

"Really?"

"Mind telling me what's so interesting?" he motioned toward the paper with his thumb.

I got the pitch right away. "Somebody else been reading up?"

He nodded, his face expressionless.

There are ways you can play people and ways you can't and this one I decided to play straight. I said, "I'm Phil Rocca. You might have heard of me. I took a big fall eight years ago and right now I'm trying to catch up."

His eyebrows furrowed. "Rocca," he mused. "Rocca . . . sure, I remember that trial. I was with a sheet in Boston then. Hell, yes, I remember you. What are you doing here?"

"It was a bum rap, friend. I'm out to prove it. It might seem silly, but I'd like to get back in the field again and the only way I can do it is to shove that rap where it belongs. That whole deal was wrapped up in Rhino Massley and I'm trying to pick it apart. Rhino's big club that kept him on top was some damn hot evidence that kept key people in line. When Rhino died he left it somewhere, and that, buddy, I'd like to come up with."

I grinned at him and let him have some more. Oh, not too much. If it ever broke it was going to be my story, or at least something I could sell or bargain with. But I leaked enough to make Stack's eyes go a little bright at the thought of what could come out of the thing.

When I finished I asked, "Who else was after the paper?"

"A local boy. He's new in town and hasn't got a record, but word came in that he's a representative for the big ones on either coast. We don't know what's in the works, but we know he's got something going for him. As soon as two people asked for the same issue, Carey over there buzzed me upstairs. Now, what's the poop?"

"Hoyt was Rhino Massley's personal physician."

"Yeah, I remember. He has some mob connections back east. He never had an outside practice here at all."

Then I pointed to the interesting part. "The friend who was killed in the same wreck is listed as having been a prominent mortician here in town."

Stack pulled the paper over to him and scanned the item. "Uh-huh. I knew him slightly. Close-mouthed guy who started up after the war. What about him?"

"Any way of finding out who did the embalming on Rhino's body?"

His eyes pulled tight, then he nodded and got up. He spent a few minutes at the phone down the end then came back and sat down. "It was him. Leo Grant. Rhino's doctor and mortician were both killed in the same wreck."

"Unusual?"

He shrugged. "Not so. Their fields are related, they worked together with the same patient, they could have been friends."

"Any way of finding out?"

"Possibly. I'll try. How does it matter?"

"Let's say that you come up with the answer, and I'll tell you how it matters. Fair enough?"

He flipped a card from his pocket and handed it to me. "You can get me at any of those three numbers. And look, where are you staying?"

"No place yet, but I'll find a flop."

"Then try the Blue Sky Motel. Harry Coleman is a friend of mine and will treat you right. You on wheels?"

"No."

He picked the card from my hand, scribbled something on it, and handed it back. "Take it to the Mermak garage. They'll rent you wheels without breaking your back."

"Thanks."

There was no hitch in getting a car. I picked a two-year-old Ford, paid out three days in advance, got directions from the clerk to the Blue Sky Motel, and drove out to meet Harry Coleman. He was a big, genial guy tanned to his elbows and neck, but otherwise, like most of the natives, a sun-dodger. He put me in a duplex all the way down the row of buildings, brought me a paper, a cold can of beer, and some ice.

I wondered if I could do it or not. One lousy drink could have set me off anytime a week ago. Somehow now it was different, and sooner or later I was going to have to find out.

It went down just right. It tasted good and was just enough. I looked at myself in the mirror and winked.

Then I flopped down on the bed and let the sleep ooze over me.

When I woke up I called the desk and found out that it was 7:30 and that I had wasted the whole afternoon.

Before I left I got the operator and gave her Terry's hotel in New York. We got right through and she answered on the second ring with a querulous "Yes?"

"Phil, honey."

"Oh, Phil!" She caressed my name the way no one else ever had. "Are you in Phoenix?"

"Here and working, kitten."

"What did you find out?" She said it almost breathlessly and waited for my answer.

"Nothing I can put in logical sequence yet. I've got some ideas but they'll have to keep."

"Phil" . . . and now she sounded worried, "you will be careful, won't you?"

"Don't worry about me, kid. Now, how did you make out? Anything on Harris?"

"Well, I went to several places and in three of them she was recognized at once. She had had a stage career right after high school, went through nurse's training and, instead of going into a hospital, went back to the stage. She had numerous small Broadway parts, several minor Hollywood things, and some TV work. Between engagements she served as a nurse in several hospitals but would give up nursing immediately for a stage part."

"Did anyone know where she could be found?"

"No, the last address they had on her was Phoenix. In fact, one agency wanted her very badly for a part. I even tried the unions and a press agent from Hollywood who was here in town, but she's dropped completely out of sight."

I let it run through my mind for a minute, then said, "Okay, kid, you did fine. Now stay put until I get back and keep checking on that contact at the Sherman."

"How long will you be there, Phil?"

"Another day at least. Can you hang on?"

"As long as I know I have you."

I grinned at the phone and threw her a kiss. "You have me, baby. I just hope you know what you're doing."

She said so-long with a kiss of her own and hung up.

I had a fine Mexican supper at the Sign of the Gaudy Parrot and found out what I needed to know by asking just one question . . . where Rhino Massley's old place was. In a small way he was a local legend for having left his place to a polio research foundation.

His old ranch was in the long shadows of the mountains, a compact group of buildings built to give a western touch to modern design. At the main building I blew my horn until lights came on from inside, then went up on the porch and waited. The man who opened the door was bald and in his 70s and not at all friendly like the bunch back in town. He looked me up and down and in no uncertain voice said, "What the hell you want?"

I let a laugh rumble around in my throat, then pushed the door open and squeezed inside, "Hello, Buster," I said.

The gun he was trying to clear from the back of his pants came loose and dangled from his hand. The skin on his face pulled tight until wrinkles showed in his scalp. "How come you make me?"

"Easy enough, Buster. You want the whole rundown just to show you how much I know?"

"Knock it off." His voice was real uncertain this time.

Buster Lafarge was one of the old-time killers from the roaring '20s. He was wanted by three states and the Feds and I personally knew five people who would pay 100 grand to have old Buster delivered alive to their private basements for old times' sake.

I held out my hand. "The heater, friend."

It was strictly his kind of rod, a big blue Army .45 that could knock a horse down. He laid it in my hand and I could feel him shaking when he touched me. All the toughness has gone out of him long ago. He was old now, too old to fight and just old enough to want to hang on to the last inch life had to give him.

He said, "Pal . . . look, I . . . I . . ."

"What're you doing here, Buster?"

"Pal. . . ."

"I can make money on you, you know that," I said. "I could drop you now and take a payoff or bring you in still kicking."

This time his voice came out in a dry rasp. "Jeez, pal, what'd I do? I don't know you. Look, pal . . ."

"What're you doing here?" I repeated.

Buster's shoulders sagged with the weight of the load he carried. "Rhino . . . he gimme the job here. They got to keep me on here. It's in his will. Jeez, pal. . . ."

"What do you do?"

"Nothing. What the hell can I do? I can't go no place. So I sweep up and paint some and keep the yard clean and make sure Rhino's grave is okay and that's all."

"Where's this grave you take care of?"

"West. About a quarter of a mile. By the palm grove."

"Good. Get a couple of shovels, Buster."

"What for?"

"We're going to dig old Rhino up, that's what for."

Very slowly he backed away from me, his eyes wide. "Man, you're plain crazy. Nuts. You got bats!"

"Out," I said. "Shovels."

A thick cluster of palms smothered the grave with a protective apron, screening it from casual eyes. The ground was flat, like a putting green and, instead of the ornate headstone I expected, a small bronze plaque on a marble backing nestled in the grass. The inscription was as simple as the setting. From overhead the light of night filtered through the gently moving fronds of the palms giving the place a peculiar life of its own.

I made Lafarge spread-eagle himself on the ground while I dug so I could keep him in sight, and when I was halfway down I threw him the shovel and made him get into the hole. He was caught between me on top and Rhino below and with every shovel full of dirt he tossed up came a whining moan broken with an occasional sob. He was a miserable slob, but in his time he had put enough people into the same kind of hole he was in now, and I wasn't wasting any sympathy on him at all.

He was completely out of sight, handing me the shovel with every stroke to throw the dirt up, when he hit the coffin. Even in the darkness I could sense what came over him, a sudden terror too great to call out, too big to run away from. He turned his head up slowly, the whites of his eyes almost fluorescent in the black pit of the grave.

I said, "Scrape it clean."

Mechanically, he went to clearing off the box-like affair that covered the casket, each motion forced, each moment bringing Lafarge closer to that one second of supreme terror.

In a way it was laughable. Lafarge who had been afraid of no man and who had killed many with his own hand was shaking with fear of meeting one who could do nothing to him at all. Nothing.

I had to jump in the hole to help him tear the boards off to expose the coffin. They were pulpy rotten with time, smelling of mold, and came up easily. Then there was old Rhino Massley's last bed and I had the point of the shovel banging into the edge until it broke loose.

And now I'd know the answer.

I carved a niche into the wall and made Lafarge stand in it while I climbed out. He looked like a shrunken-up gnome standing there, shivering silently at the thought of what I was going to make him do.

"Open it," I said.

His voice was barely audible. "No. Please, Mac . . . no."

He heard the hammer of the .45 come back and it was enough. His whine turned into jerky sobs and he reached for the lid of the coffin. Twice it slipped from his fingers, then with a convulsive heave he had it open and when I struck the match he took one look at what was inside, gagged with sheer fright, and collapsed in a faint that jammed the lid wide open.

Rhino Massley's body was a bag of sand.

It was a heady feeling knowing I had been right. The excitement was pounding in my chest and head, making my ears ring. I laughed out loud right where I stood and the sound of it was just enough to cover up the sudden rush of feet until it was too late.

The first one got me across the back of the neck, then struck again across the skull. I yelled, tried to get up, but there were others on me then. I was half over the edge of the open grave when a gun roared in my ears and below me somebody let out a pitiful wail. Then it was my head again and I was falling into the pit myself, the one I helped dig with my own hands.

It hit across the thing in the bottom without feeling, a

strange and new sensation like being dead, I thought. I could still hear sounds, the yells of men, and twice the hollow reverberations like far off thunder. Then as suddenly as it happened the numbness of that brief half life was swept away on a sea of pain.

Above me somebody said, "Rocca . . . hey, Rocca . . ." and a shaft of light flooded the grave.

It hurt, but I propped an arm under me and pushed up.

"He's okay. Can you take care of those two, Johnny?"

Another voice said, "They're not going any place."

There was a scrambling into the hole, a long drawn-out whistle as the person realized what was there, then hands hooked under my armpits and dragged me to my feet.

"You all right?"

The light swept over me and in its beam I saw Joe Stack, the front of him covered with dirt and blood trickling down one side of his face.

I nodded. "I'm okay." I spit out the taste of mold and wiped my mouth with the back of my hand. "Lafarge?"

Joe turned the light on the open end of the coffin. It was partially filled now by a sandbag and a man, and there was no difference between either because all both were, was dirt. A bullet had nearly taken the top of Lafarge's head off and the cycle for him was complete.

The .45 was half covered by dirt and I didn't leave it there. I picked it up, and without bothering to clean it, shoved it under my belt out of sight.

Joe said, "Ready to go up?"

"Sure."

He gave me a hoist and I sprawled on the mound of dirt we had thrown up, the sudden, stunning pain in the back of my head tearing down the muscles of my back and into my legs. Another light was going over me, taking in every detail, the reflection of it bouncing off the one who held it, a tall, heavyset guy with blood on his face.

"This is the one?"

I heard Joe answer, "That's him."

"He's got plenty to talk about."

My head was clearing again. I managed to get to my knees, then on my feet. I felt myself grinning foolishly at the big guy. "Who're you?"

"Police. You were lucky, mister."

He flashed the light down beside him. The two motionless shadows I had assumed to be mounds of dirt turned into men, handcuffed back to back.

"There was another one," the cop said. "He got away."

"Put your light back on them."

The beam of the flash traced a path to their heads. "Know them?"

I nodded. "One. He's a hood named Joe Coon who works for Mannie Waller in New York. The other one is new to me."

"He's local. Been here for a couple of years. Tough punk who has a small record but a big reputation. We've always pegged him for a hired gun for the L.A. bunch."

"What about the other one?"

I felt the cop shrug. "We heard his car. He took off."

"That's great."

"Why sweat. These two will talk. We'll pick him up."

Joe Stack said, "Let's not make it easy for him. Suppose I get back to town with Rocca here and get your office to work."

The cop hesitated and I saw him scowl. "I don't like it."

"Listen, Johnny, you wouldn't have tied into this one at all if I didn't steer you to it. I tried to tell you this was different and you should have seen enough to know this is hot. Now throw it through channels and you'll blow the ass right off the bit. Either play it the way I suggested or lose it and look like a fool. I know what Rocca's bumping. Don't louse him up or he won't be telling you or anybody else anything and, as far as I'm concerned, I don't blame him."

"Damn it, Stack, he'll talk too, if I want him to!"

Joe's breath came in with a hiss. "Don't rub me, Johnny. I'm from the Fourth Estate, remember?"

"He's not."

"Like hell. He is as of right now. If he wants, I'm putting him on my staff. How do you like them apples?"

The cop grunted, shook his head, and scowled. "Okay, Chief Bigheart, I'll go along. Sometimes it's better this way. Take the car and send out Aldridge and Garcia. How much time are you going to need?"

Stack glanced in my direction. I said, "What time is it?"

"Almost 10:30."

"We'll have something in the morning."

"It better be something for me, friend."

"You aren't alone," I told him. "This isn't local."

"Okay, I'm a sucker. I'm lucky I have 20 years in without any strikes. This could cost me."

Stack took my arm. "Let's go. Can you make it to the house?"

"If we don't run."

"Jokes yet he tells," the cop said.

Stack made the call to Aldridge and Garcia from his own office.

When he hung up I put down the almost-finished highball he made up for me and took the towel off my head.

"Fine. Now cut me in," I said. "You were there at the grave like gangbusters."

"I gave you the Mermak and the Blue Sky Motel so I could stay with you. Man, I was on your tail ever since you left the building here. Now let's hear your side. Where did the boys come from?"

"I thought about it all the way back. Before I left New York I got creamed in the men's room of the airfield. I thought it was for some loot, but that was a cover. Somebody sapped me, took a look at my airline ticket in time to get on the same plane. That was buddy Joe Coon. He was the one I told you about."

"That Mannie Waller deal?"

I nodded.

"Back in New York the word is going out fast. Rhino Massley isn't dead at all. His grave is empty. Ten to one the lad who got away put in a fast phone call to the office."

"So what's the next step?"

I pointed to his desk. "Can I use the phone?"

"Be my guest."

I picked up the receiver, dialed the operator and gave her the number of the Enfield Hotel, person-to-person to Terry. The hotel PBX rang for a full minute, then gave me a DA. Nobody answered. I cancelled the call and put in another to Dan Litvak, at Rooney's.

"Where are you?" he asked.

"Phoenix."

"Oh? What's with Rhino Massley?"

"Rhino's grave was empty. He's not dead."

"It's your deal, kid. Go on."

"Swell! Now do you think you can influence Cal Porter to start some action on this thing?"

"Like how?"

I told him what happened back at Rhino's old place and listened to him let out a long low hiss. I said, "Give it to Porter straight, but don't let him start blowing any whistles. First have him check the State Department and steamship lines for anything on Elena Harris, Rhino's former nurse. The date would be shortly after he supposedly died. Okay. Then see if you can run down the Harris dame wherever she is. The paper ought to foot the phone calls."

"That's it then?"

"Maybe you can lean on Porter a little bit. Make sure he has somebody on Waller from here on in. If there's a political rub, he might want to play it cool."

I hung up. Stack was looking at me with a little grin. "Don't be giving anything away, friend. You're on the staff now, remember?" He handed me a fresh drink across the table and I took it mechanically. Without realizing it I held it in my hand a long minute before raising it to my mouth and when I did it was the full realization that the old compulsion was gone completely.

I said, "Joe, this story has two ends. One in New York and one here. It's an old story and I've been in it since the beginning. I want in on it at the end. The story is big enough for a couple of papers, but I'm not doing it for the sake of a news scoop. I've been a patsy long enough. There are a lot of eyes I'd like to have look my way again. Until now I haven't realized how much I'd like to have my integrity restored and proven."

"I have something to show you." He slid a folder across the desk. "File on Massley. Most of it's local. What was this thing he had about dames?"

"Beats me. He didn't take to anybody except his nurse."

"You're not kidding. You know he had three assault charges brought against him by three different housekeepers?"

"When he was in the lung?"

"On two occasions, when he was out of it for the few minutes necessary, he took the time to belt one woman with an ash tray and hit the other with a bottle of rubbing alcohol. After all the verbal abuse they took from Rhino that finished it. Both of them dropped the charges after an out-of-court settlement."

"Who was the third?"

"A newspaper woman. She was outside his window with a camera and he fired right through the window at her."

"What's your point?"

"It's an old story. He's had charges like these flung at him a dozen times. Anything there?"

I shrugged, took another small pull at the drink and pushed it away from me. It was no trouble to do it at all. "Nothing I can touch at the moment. It's a peculiar facet of his personality I found out about back home. Why this interest?"

"Because on everything else he was clean. Massley apparently went to every extent to keep in the background. He was legal, at least on the surface. He ran a neat, efficient organization and let as little trouble touch him as possible. Then this stuff pops up. He's gone after more dames with his hands or anything available than you can count. Each time he has to go out of his way to clear the deal with a handful of dough."

"So he hates dames."

"Not his nurse."

"There is always the exception," I said. I stood up and pushed the phone at him. "Call the airport and see who you know. I want a flight out."

He made a tight face. "The cops are going to want to talk to you."

"You talk for me."

"You're the one with the story. What can I say?"

"Maybe something about how peculiar it was that the

doctor who signed Massley's death certificate and the mortician who embalmed him died in a supposed accident together right after the funeral that was held for a bag of sand. Hell, they ought to be glad they got the two who creamed Lafarge."

"That's one story they'll want everything on."

"Guardian of a buried sandbag," I told him. "As long as nobody dug the coffin up, Rhino was safe some place. Those hoods who jumped me got the idea real fast and didn't want the information spread around. If you didn't show up, Lafarge and I would have filled that hole and if they handled it right nobody would have been wised up."

The DC8B landed short, slowed up on its brakes and turned into the first taxi strip. As it swung onto the apron I saw them, the unmistakables, men stamped by their jobs. The pair of two-tone patrol cars would not have been the giveaway, if they hadn't backed up the black sedan with the small mid-roof antenna.

Cops. Liaison between Phoenix and New York must have been excellent.

Cal Porter wasn't taking any chances on me running off with a hatful of information that could make him governor. At least I should have expected it. You don't keep murder quiet. At least not too inexpensively.

The cop met me at the foot of the ramp, took my arm, and tried to steer me. I said, "Lay off."

For a second it looked like he was going to have fun, then Cal Porter was there, smiling pleasantly just in case, another plainclothesman behind him. "Phoenix called, Rocca."

"It's what I expected, Porter."

The cop nudged me. "Say mister."

I gave him the old two words and turned to the D.A. "Lay off me, Porter. Treat me like a slob and it's going to look like you fell through the crapper. I'm past being pushed, especially by you. From now on you stay on the safe side, not me. You pulled the cork eight years ago, but it won't happen now." I looked around at the nice assemblage, well-trained and efficient, all there to do it the way the book said, no matter what it cost anybody else.

I said, "You got one stinking chance to play it smart,

Porter. I won't give you two at all. If you spoke to Phoenix, you know there's a press working on my side this time without a publisher like Gates who let his men get thrown to the dogs.

"Maybe you know that I got time working for me and, if I don't talk, then you'll look like the most stupid idiot that ever faced a court and, brother, will I call the names out. In fact, come to think of it, you haven't got a damn thing to say at all. Not a god damn thing. So toss me in the slammer and I'll wait it out. I'll wait until it's over with, then shove it into you and break it off."

The plainclothesman said, "Want me to calm him down, Mr. Porter?"

Cal was white. His nostrils were pinched and turning green from pressure, but he shook his head. He waved his hand absently at the cops. "You men go back. Mr. Rocca here will go with me." He let the rage seep out of his face slowly. "That all right with you, Mr. Rocca?"

"Certainly, Mr. Porter," I said. "Has Dan filled you in on the details?"

"He has. Now we'll see what you have to say, Mr. Rocca."

We met Dan Litvak in Rooney's. He was alone in a booth, the ash tray littered with souvenirs of his wait. His face was carefully expressionless, but I knew what he was thinking. When Cal Porter sat down opposite him, he said, "You didn't play it wisely, Cal."

"So I learned. Maybe I can still smarten up."

Dan glanced up, thought about it, and smiled slowly. He reached in his pocket and took out a folded sheaf of papers covered with his own type of shorthand. "Between Cal and me, we have that information on Elena Harris."

I tried to keep the quaver out of my voice when I told him to spill it.

"Elena Harris booked passage for Rio two weeks after Rhino died."

"Supposedly died," I cut in.

He nodded. "Supposedly. She has been in Rio since and has been the constant companion of an unidentified gentleman known only as Richard Castor. This man joined her about the time she arrived and until a few months ago . . . well, you know how it gets."

"Yeah . . . sure."

"So Castor dropped out of sight. Meantime the Harris woman has been cutting a wide swath through local Latin society. She's a blonde and they go for blondes there, especially the ones with class."

"And Castor . . ."

"At this point, is missing," Dan said.

"No history at all?"

Dan shrugged. "All this came over the phone, but he had a beard, was distinguished, and had plenty of loot. The only trouble he got into was when he had a brawl with a couple of women. He beat both of them up pretty badly."

"Rhino," I said quietly. "It's him."

Cal Porter tapped the table with his fingers. "We caught the business with the women too." His fingers stopped the tapping and he looked at me. "Are you ready to talk?"

"In a minute. What's with Mannie Waller?"

"We can't locate him . . . yet. Several of his men are under surveillance and all his known hangouts are covered." He paused, coughed into his hand, and said, "He's pretty big now."

"How big?"

"Outsized. We didn't realize to what extent until we went to town on him. Mannie Waller, for all his crassness, is probably the Syndicate's *Mr. Big*. Since Appalachin they've played it plenty cute."

"And he disappeared right after I opened Rhino's grave."

"Apparently."

"The call got through then."

"That's right. Now supposing, since we're all in this nice informal atmosphere, you say what's on your mind. If I didn't feel like you had a possibility of being right, and on top of that, that it could have been me who sent you away for seven years on a bum rap, you wouldn't be getting this opportunity to make me look like a fool. And if Dan didn't go along with you, I don't think I would have either. But now you're getting your chance. Just lay it out so we can see what it is."

I sat back, put the pieces together the way it looked best and gave them the picture.

"Before I was sent up I made a project out of Rhino Massley, intending to get hold of the documented evidence that determined his position inside the organization he ran and the outside loot to go with it. You know what happened. I took too big a bite. Rhino managed a neatly setup frame and I took a dive behind bars. And with me gone Rhino was riding high . . . nobody big enough to push or cut him out. He had it made, but then came a time when he wanted out of the organization and things like this just don't happen unless you kick off.

"Buddy Rhino met Elena Harris and fell like a ton of bricks. She had show-girl looks, was educated, had everything Rhino ever wanted, and he went off the deep end. She had one other thing, too. She was a nurse, and this could have given him the idea. He cooked up a way to get out of the mob, without a sword hanging over his neck, and open up a new life for himself.

"So he fakes this polio thing. He went through the whole iron lung act because who the hell would think anybody would fake that? Suicide or murder maybe, but never anything like that. He even waited until a storm cut the power on the lung to make it look real. His nurse couldn't get the auxiliary power started in time.

"The doctor was fixed, of course. So was the mortician. They both thought they were made for life for their part in it and in a way they were. Rhino bumped them himself and made it look like an accident. He even managed to hold still in a casket for some photos and made it look good.

"He was the Syndicate paymaster and he had a bundle. He was supposed to keep it well hidden, so when he died suddenly and the bank was never uncovered, the mob simply felt that he had done his job a little too well, discounted the loss, and started fresh. At that point Rhino and Elena took off for Rio, he under an assumed name and properly disguised."

I paused there and waited. Dan was doodling idly on the edge of paper. Cal Porter said, "It's making sense. Go on."

"Now I speculate. Rio was a little too rich. Elena got

out of hand. Those millionaires down there have an income at least. All of Rhino's loot was going out. It wouldn't take too many bad turns of the card to have that happen. Finally Rhino was wiped out and Elena wasn't holding still for it. She dumped Rhino for somebody else and the big act was all for nothing."

I could feel the scowl on Porter's face as he reached for the events and tried to sift them.

I said, "But to get back . . . Rhino's original hold on the mob itself and its outside agencies was his 'black bundle,' the stuff that could crucify plenty of big ones in and out of government. If it were a buried secret like the mob presumed the money to be, everything was all right.

"After all, during the time Rhino was gone it never turned up and it could be counted as being out of existence. In a way, it was almost like that. He had that hidden well . . . it had gone with his ex-wife so completely nobody could run it down. Then one day the ex-wife died and it came out quite inadvertently who she was and the mob was onto a new lead. There was the possibility that Rhino had separated the money and his 'package,' leaving the latter where it was accessible yet hidden.

"The mob couldn't afford not to follow up this idea. They suspected that Rhino's *black bundle* could have been among her effects. The survivor was Rhino's daughter, Terry, and as such inherited. The mob watched and waited and when Terry suddenly came to New York, they thought they had it pinned down. . . . Terry Massley had Rhino's stuff and was coming in to make a sale. Like father, like daughter, they figured. They laid for her, most likely figuring to make her talk, or if she wouldn't, knock her off and conduct a search themselves. By coincidence, I got involved."

The D.A.'s face seemed frozen. "By sheer coincidence," he repeated.

"Drop dead," I said.

"This coincidence is pretty far fetched," Porter remarked sourly. "This *black bundle* of Massley's was the invisible factor in Rocca's trial. Now suddenly by coincidence the girl runs into him."

Dan laughed. "You know what you should call this coincidence, Cal?"

Reluctantly, Porter asked, "What?"

"Luck. It's going to make you governor."

Then it was my turn. "That is," I said, "if I don't squawk about that bum rap I took back there."

The knuckles of Porter's fingers showed white. "I'm not making any deals. All I want to do is play it right."

"Me too, Mr. Porter, me too. I want it right. It's just that I have something coming to me for those seven years and I intend to get it."

"We'll talk about it. What do you want?"

"Legwork. You have everything going for you, so you might be able to get L.A. to process Rhino's ex-wife's effects. She left something behind that hasn't been uncovered and we have to find it first."

Porter scribbled something on a pad and nodded. I waved for the waiter, told him to bring a phone, and dialed the Enfield Hotel. After a minute the operator informed me that Terry wasn't in her room. I hung up scowling and Dan wanted to know what the matter was. "Terry's not around. She wasn't there when I called from Phoenix."

"You know how dames are."

"I told her to stay put."

"For two days? You're nuts. She's around the hotel some place. Have her paged."

"No," I said, "I'm going up there myself. I don't want to broadcast anything." I looked at Cal Porter. "Okay with you . . . or did Phoenix put a hold order on me?"

For the first time Cal let a smile show. "They would have liked to. In fact, over somebody's protestations out there, they suggested it. You stirred up a big one."

"You'll do the stirring if you can get somebody to really shake down the late Mrs. Massley's effects out there."

Dan flipped another cigarette into his mouth. "And what do I do, boss man?" he grinned.

"More legwork. See if you can get anybody to identify Richard Castor as having shipped out of Rio bound for the States. I doubt if he would have travelled first class."

Both of them were watching me closely now.

I said, "I think Rhino Massley slipped back here intending to pick up his old documents in order to finance another bankroll to buy Elena Harris back with. I think it was Massley who contacted Terry, knowing that some-where in her mother's effects was his big hope."

Porter nodded curtly. "There's only one hole."

We both waited for it.

"Rhino's got a crazy fixation *against* women. Then suddenly he's all gone over this Harris girl?"

It was something that had bothered me too, but I dis-missed it with the only thing I could think of. "There's an exception to every rule, Mr. Porter. Meanwhile, it's the only line of reasoning we have."

I let them think about it, told them I'd call back later and walked out.

The maid was a short, doughty old woman, and she was certain about it. She didn't quibble or hedge and the fin I had given her hadn't bought a story. The girl in my room who had registered in as my wife wasn't there and hadn't been all day. Previously she wouldn't let anyone in, even to make up the room. Twice the day before, room service had brought in a tray, but that was all. However, this morning when the maid had tried the door with her master key since there was no Do Not Disturb sign out and the door was not locked from inside, she went in, cleaned up, and went out.

Then, for some oblique reason of her own, she asked, "Your wife, was it?" and when I nodded curtly she made a universal grimace, the superior smile of those who know. She thought, too, she knew why the fin and why my questions and said quickly, "She gave quite a party, mister, I'll say that. There were cigar butts around and the room was all pulled apart."

I said thanks and let it drop there. I couldn't have said more because my throat was tight with a cold fear. I went back inside and opened the drawers of the dresser. Her things were there, carelessly thrown around, showing all the signs of having been hurriedly searched. Deliberately, I checked every spot in the room, but the things I was looking for, her mother's personal effects, weren't there.

Terry was gone. Why? There had been men here. Why? Yet, I knew some of these things. Like the men. It's surprising how great a force the unlawful comprise. They had men to do the legwork, money to buy pieces of knowledge, experience to follow up the slightest detail. And they had a motive. Mannie Waller's men had been here, all right. I let the picture of it run through my mind, then it stopped being quite so grim. They were here and left, but not with Terry, otherwise there would have been no cigar butts or careless searches.

I picked up the phone, settled the whole thing on my lap, and lifted the receiver. And even as I was giving the desk clerk Dan Litvak's number I saw the note. She had stuck it under the phone base itself and all that time it had stayed there, hidden until now. Very simply it read:

Darling, I was contacted at the Sherman and the arrangement is almost the same as before. This time I was to carry mother's personal items in the identifying suitcase, but rather than that I'm leaving them in your hole in the wall. Don't worry. I'll be all right. Love you.

Terry.

The idiot? What the hell gets into women that they think they can walk head-on into men playing guns and walk right out again! My hands shook so that I could hardly hold the phone and when Dan finally came on the same shake was back in my voice.

I said, "Terry's gone. Rhino made his contact."

"You sure it was Rhino?"

"That's what I'm calling for. You have anything on Castor?"

"Not yet. Now what about Terry?"

I gave him the picture quickly as far as I saw it. "Suppose I pass this on to Cal. He'll want to go all out on it."

"Go to it. I'll see if I can find Terry."

"How?"

"She said the arrangements were almost the same as before. Rhino is some place in my neighborhood and she's to meet him there. There's nobody I don't know around home plate and, if Terry has been there, somebody would have spotted her. If she goes through with this contact and comes out of it, she'll try to reach me either here or at my pad on the street. Give me two hours and we'll all meet at my place. Got that?"

"Yeah, but how about you taking some help along."

"No dice, kid. A team would be spotted too fast. Me those people will talk to. Anybody else, nix. And if they think I'm working with cops they'll clam up on me, too. We have to play it like this."

"Okay then. If that's how you call it. See you later. Watch it."

I said I would and hung up.

Once it began, night came on with a desperate rush. Over the city the belly-rumbling of the storm to the west closed the shops early.

I had walked the street from Seventh to the river, then back again, questioning those who would know if anyone would, asking them, in turn, to question others. Yes, Terry had been seen, all right, by two persons next to my own building. She came to my place, stayed a few minutes, and left. Where she went to, or where she was now, nobody could tell me.

There wasn't any sense going to my apartment now. All she did was leave those meaningless things of her mother's in my trick closet, the hole in the wall she first hid in. How long ago? Years . . . months? It hardly seemed like days.

So I kept on asking, people in doorways, the paperman on the corner, the kids, the hack drivers waiting just off the avenues. They were nice, they were sympathetic, but they couldn't help.

And when the rain started I turned up my collar and gave up. Inside me I had that terrible disjointed feeling that comes with a hangover and your nervous signals get all crossed until you're ready to scream with despair. I walked back to my apartment, went in, closed the door and reached to switch on the light.

I needn't have bothered. Somebody else did it for me.

Mannie Waller, fat and ugly looking, squatting on the couch, said, "We only had to wait, wise guy. Sooner or later you'd come back to your hole in the wall, all right." The three with him just smiled. Big smiles.

He glanced around, his nose wrinkled in disgust. I followed his eyes, looking at the wreckage of the place, the broken chairs, the upturned drawers, the litter from the pillow and mattress. I couldn't help grinning, though. It was a lousy joke, but still a joke. Mannie was thinking about the wrong hole in the wall.

What a sucker I turned out to be. Sure, Mannie had seen Terry's note. He had even left it there for me to see too, and if I had, I would have come roaring over like a white knight and been roasted in my own armor. The cleaning woman in the hotel had probably covered up Terry's note inadvertently, and I had assumed that only I saw it.

"It's funny?" Mannie asked. "Show him it ain't funny, Ruby."

I tried to cover up but I wasn't quick enough. A gun barrel raked the back of my scalp and I went down on my knees with the sticky warmth of blood soaking into my collar.

"Where is it, wise guy?"

"Like . . . what . . ."

Mannie nodded sagely. "I spell it out just once. What the kid has. The stuff. Rhino's stuff. She left it here."

My breath was coming in hard. The guy called Ruby nudged me with a toe and said, "Another one, Mannie?"

I shook my head. "Wait. I'll . . . tell you."

"Give him a minute, Ruby."

How long? How long did I have? I managed to get a foot under me and poised there breathing deeply, in a runner's stance. The blood from my head ran down and dripped off my chin making it look better still. Then when I had milked it as long as I could I came off the floor with a wild shriek stinging my own ears.

My fist caught Mannie flush in the face and I felt bone and teeth go into a splintery mess. The one beside him reached for me as I turned and I almost put my foot through his genitals. Someone swung a gun again and missed, smashing it into my shoulder. My entire side went numb, my knees collapsed, and even on the way down the fists and the feet started their torture. I rolled on one side, gagging on the blood in my mouth, the sudden retching clearing my head, and for one second I cursed myself for a damn fool because all that time I had Lafarge's gun stuck under my belt and never thought to use it.

But thinking of it then was enough. The one hand under me snaked it out of its own volition and when I rolled over my face was exposed and the one called Ruby laughed and brought his foot back to kick it off.

Then I pulled the trigger and it was Ruby's face that disappeared and the last thing I saw was his hat flying toward the ceiling as his head exploded. A foot shocked me almost senseless and my eyes closed.

Mannie's voice was far away, a horrible mumbling, swearing at the other two. Dimly, I heard one say, "How the hell could we know?"

"You jerks," Mannie sobbed. "I should kill you. Look at Ruby."

"Who figures him for rods, Mannie. Hell, Mannie . . ."

"Shut up. You take care of him. Right now, you hear? Then we blow. You get yours later, you jerks!"

"Sure, Mannie, sure." The metallic click of the hammer of a gun coming back was louder than all the other sounds. It was like a crashing cymbal stroke next to my ear. The guy said, "I'll put him in cold storage, good, Mannie."

Too late the warmth of knowledge reached me. Too late, from those few words, did the answer stand out, stark and simple. Too late did I finally understand the reasoning of a woman, untrained in the devious, thinking only in her natural manner. How much blood, how many dead, how much more to go because the entire affair was overly simplified?

I could feel myself trying to withdraw from what was coming, my brain pleading for a numbed body to move, to hide. But the body could do neither. The brain heard the smashing thunder of the shots and with a terrible effort forced the body to twitch, to feel out the pain.

There were more rolling thunders and loud voices and again the brain cried out to move . . . MOVE! When I did hands went under me, sat me up, and a voice I knew was Dan's said, "Phil! Phil! You all right?"

My eyes came open, focused, and I nodded.

Behind him was Cal Porter and two plainclothesmen, each with a gun in his hand. Cal had gone white and I knew he was ready to be sick. Ruby was dead where I had shot him, two more sprawled out lifelessly across him. Mannie was blubbering insanely on the couch, his eyes huge and wild, his voice trying to come through a swollen mass of flesh that was his mouth.

Dan said, "What happened . . . but don't talk if you're hurt."

"I'm . . . okay." I pointed to the closet and told Porter to open it. He found the catch, swung the door out, and picked up the box from the floor. He found the wallet, emptied it into his hands and looked at me.

I said, "Receipts for clothes . . . in cold storage. Look at . . . the date. They've been there for . . . years."

"Go on."

"Rhino's wife . . . hid the stuff there. A damn woman's . . . trick. Get to a phone. Check on it . . . and you'll be governor, Mr. Porter."

Dan hoisted me to my feet. "I have to call this story in. We can't keep it quiet now." He looked at the door and nodded. The crowd had already gathered, staring, gasping, speculating. The two cops were having a job keeping them out.

I said, "A favor, friend. I hate to make you share your scoop, but you know my buddy in Phoenix?"

"Okay," Dan laughed. "He'll get it the same time."

Porter had gotten his color back. He seemed different now, the softness gone from his face, the old determination back again. "Where's the nearest phone?"

"Store on the corner."

"I'll check this out." He smiled gently, trying for a degree of friendliness. "I have a feeling, you know what I mean?"

"I know. The stuff will be there." I put my hand on his arm. "Look," I told him. "No hard feelings. Things go wrong sometimes."

Outside a siren wailed, stopped in front of the buildings, and two uniformed cops came in with guns drawn. Porter gave Mannie over to them, left instructions with the others, and he turned to me with a final wave.

I went out in the hall behind him. The cops had squeezed everybody out the front door and were standing there waving them off. The little Gomez boy didn't bother coming in that way. He came up through the cellar and said very softly from behind me, "Meestair Phil?"

I turned around. "Oh, hello, kid."

"You look for the nice lady. Pretty lady with black hair? She who was here?"

My mouth was suddenly dry and I nodded.

"I see something, Meestair Phil. I don't tell nobody before. I no want trouble."

"What was it, kid?"

"You know Leavy's store?"

"Sure."

"By the side an alley?"

I nodded, remembering the place. "It was boarded up."

"No. Not boards. Somebody take down soon ago."

"Okay, no boards."

The kid looked around as though he were fearful of being overheard. "Thees pretty lady. She has bag." He stretched his hands apart showing me how big it was. "Like so. She walk down street and man come out. Thees man he very mad and he pull her inside. I hear her yell."

Without knowing it I had the kid by the shoulder shaking him. "Damn it, what happened?"

Sudden fear came into his eyes and he stiffened. I let him go, forced a smile and waited. He shrugged, swallowed, and said, "I do not go in there, Meestair Phil. I no want trouble."

"No trouble, kid." I reached in my pocket and took out a bill. The kid clutched at it like a miracle come true, grinned broadly, and darted off toward the darkness of the cellar. I walked back to the room where the bodies were, found Lafarge's .45 on the floor and shoved it back under my belt. Then I went out the way the kid had gone out, past the cops, the curious, onto a street whose occupants were all clustered in front of one building.

It was raining again, the dehydrated smells of the city being activated again into a foul soup of human essence. I walked through it to the corner, thinking of how Terry had run across this same street into the same room where so much had happened only minutes ago. And now there were only a few steps left.

Like the Gomez kid said, the boards weren't there any more. I went through the gap into the blackness of an alley, my hands touching the rough brick of the building walls on either side of me. I walked slowly, feeling for debris with my feet, not knowing where I was or where I was going, knowing only that some place this alley ended and there I would find Terry.

Alive, if I weren't too late.

The alley was longer than I expected. Twice I felt the steel grilling from cellar windows under my feet and tried them, but they were rusted shut and impossible to budge. The litter of years, cans and papers and junk thrown off rooftops was thick, but curiously enough not scattered underfoot. It was as though a path had been kicked through the stuff.

That's how I knew when I reached the end of the path. A knee-high pile of garbage stopped me and when I felt the walls, in the one on my left I touched a door.

I had the .45 in my fist when I shoved it open. Unexpectedly it swung soundlessly and I stepped inside, my guts half ready to stop a bullet. My eyes were well-adjusted to the darkness and I could see as well as sense the incredible pile of junk that filled the room. It was an old storeroom of some kind, long unused. Very faintly a yellow tinge showed me the way, a path between stacked crates. I walked quietly, carefully, followed the bend in the aisle to the other door through whose time-grimed window came the pale glow of a lamp.

Inside there was the rhythmic clap of flesh on flesh and the steady cursing of a deep chested voice saying vile things over and over again.

The door was locked. Momentarily. I kicked the damn thing open and went in with a roar and in that small fraction of time saw Terry, bloody and bruised in the chair, her eyes open without seeing and the face of Rhino Massley coming at me with a hoarse yell of maniacal fury.

I should have shot him then. I shouldn't have waited. I shouldn't have let all the pent-up things boil out of my mind into my fists because he slammed into me and the gun flew out of my hand to the floor and Rhino was on top of me clawing for my throat.

There was nothing left in me, nothing at all. I was a complete fool, dead weak from the terrible things that happened to me at the apartment and I couldn't tear him off.

If Terry hadn't moaned softly then, he would have killed me. Instead he cursed her with a hiss, climbed off me, and took a step toward the table. When he turned around, he had a gun in his hand, his eyes lit up so that the white showed all around the iris and I realized that Massley was mad, completely mad.

I looked up at him, my breath coming in great sucking gasps.

"You're part of this, aren't you?" he said.

Instead of answering him I lifted my hand and pointed to Terry. "She's . . . your daughter. You did that to . . . your daughter?"

His teeth shone in the yellow light, lips bared so that his face was a lined mask of hate. "I have no daughter. Somewhere I have a son. A son. A son."

I shook my head. "Terry is. . . ."

"Terry is my son!" he shouted. "Somewhere I have a son. Damn them all. Damn all women for what they are. I have only a son, do you understand! She left me a son and named him Terry. It was he who should have carried that suitcase. Damn you both! Damn you and that woman there. What have you done with him?"

He was quieter this time, a little more rational for the moment. "You know what it is I want, otherwise you wouldn't be here."

I let my head drop with a nod of assent.

"Do you tell me or do I simply kill you and look for myself. It won't be too hard to do."

"Let her go," I whispered.

He shrugged. "Why not? She really doesn't matter."

"My apartment. Down the street. Third house from the corner. Downstairs left apartment."

"I see." He looked toward Terry, smiling peculiarly. She was breathing heavily, a trickle of blood running from her nose, but now her eyes were closed. Without looking at me, knowing I was too far away to be able to do a thing, he said, "You like this . . . woman?"

Once again, I nodded dumbly, sensing full well what he was going to do. He still watched Terry, still smiled that terrible way. And while he watched I moved my eyes and saw the .45 where it had fallen and sobbed deeply and let myself collapse again.

When I got up this time Rhino Massley was smiling, the gun in his hand pointed at Terry's head and to me he said, "Then watch her die."

I let him smile for the last time and squeezed the trigger of the .45 and watched it cave in his chest. The gun he held went off into the ceiling then flew out of his hand, but I didn't let that stop me. I disintegrated Rhino's face into a crazy welter of bits and pieces and when the last slug was gone threw the empty rod at his body and stood there yelling my head off with a panic that lasted only a minute.

The soft cry of Terry's voice spun me around. She was sitting up, the shock of the gunshots jerking her into consciousness, eyes wide with terror and one hand over her mouth covering a soundless scream.

I took her in my arms, cradled her, and let her bury her face against me. Outside I could hear the whistles and the yells and voices shouting directions.

I said, "It's all right, baby, it's all over now."

"Phil?" It was a child's question, asking for a touch of security.

"It's me, kitten. He won't hurt you ever again. It's all right." I kissed her gently, softly, knowing that now she was hurt. Later I would tell her what happened. Not all of it, nor would anyone else. There was no reason for any to know. As far as the world was concerned, Rhino was buried back there in Phoenix. Cal Porter would see to that. What he had to work with now gave him a lever big enough to pull it off or even jack himself into the big chair in Albany. It would be an easy story to tell. Simple. Rhino Massley's *black bundle* had been found. Certain hoods tried to beat the law to it and were killed.

She opened her eyes, drew back, and looked at me. She smiled through the pain she felt and touched my face. Across the room she could see the huddled lump of Massley.

"That man, Phil. He wasn't my father." Her voice had a note of surety.

"You're right, Terry. He was just another hood. He had a gimmick he thought could get you to lead him to something. He's dead."

"But my father . . . ?"

"He died a long time ago, sugar. You never knew him."

I kissed her again.

"Let's go home," I said.

And we did——

THE BASTARD BANNERMAN

CHAPTER ONE

I let the old Ford drift over the hill so I could see the sweep of the Bannerman estate nestling in the cove of the bay with the light of the full moon throwing shadows from the tall pines and making the columns of the mansion stand clear like a skeletal hand.

The hedgerow inside the fieldstone wall that surrounded the place had outgrown it by six feet since I had seen it last and as I eased past the huge brick posts that had once supported a handmade wrought iron gate I could see what time and negligence had done to it. The gates were still there, but propped open, the posts ripped loose from the brick.

At no time did I have any intention of stopping by. Cutting off the main east-west highway onto 242 was an act of curiosity more than nostalgia, but when a guy lives the first twelve years of his life in a place before he gets the boot into the wild world outside, it's a natural thing to want to see if his old home had as many scars as he did.

Through the break in the tree line I could see the lights on downstairs. I grinned to myself, braked the Ford, backed up and turned in the drive and followed the curve of it up to the house.

What a damn fool I am, I thought. *Do I shake hands or slap somebody's tail for them? This was no prodigal son returning and if I expected a happy homecoming I was blowing smoke all the way.*

But what the hell, that was all twenty-three years ago, two wars ago, a lifetime ago and when curiosity gets the better of you, go to it. Like the old man used to say before he died though, just remember what it did to the cat. Then he'd laugh because that was my name. C. C., for Cat Cay Bannerman.

Now I knew the joke. Cat Cay was where I was conceived and born, only out of wedlock. The girl died an hour after I showed up and the old man brought me home with his name and a stigma the rest of the family couldn't live with.

The *bar sinister.* The bastard Bannerman. To be raised with the *bar dexter* class in wealth and tradition, but always on the tail end out of sight so the blight on the family escutcheon wouldn't be seen by the more genteel folk.

I parked behind the two other cars, walked up the broad flight of steps to the porch and pulled the bell cord. It had an electrical device now and chimed somewhere inside. When that happened the voices that seemed a little too loud suddenly stopped and when the door opened I looked at the tiny old lady that used to make me jelly sandwiches when I was locked in my room and tell me everything was going to be all right and I said, "Hello, Annie."

She stiffened automatically, looked up at me over her glasses, annoyed. "Yes?" Her voice was thin now, and quavered a little.

I bent down and kissed her cheek. It was quick and she didn't have time to pull away, but her mouth opened in a gasp of indignation. Before she could speak I said,

"It's been a long time, Annie. Don't you remember the one you called your pussy cat?"

Her eyebrows went up slowly as memories returned. She reached out, touched my face, shaking her head in disbelief. "Cat. My little Cat Cay."

I lifted her right off her feet, held her up and squeezed her a little. The two day old beard was rough against her cheek and she squealed with a little sob of pleasure until I put her down. "I don't believe it," she told me. "So many years. You're so . . . so big now. Come in, Cat, come in, come in."

"You haven't changed, Annie. You still smell of apple pie and furniture polish."

She closed the door, took my arm with fragile fingers, stepped back and looked at me closely. "Yes, it's you all right . . . the broken nose Rudy gave you, the scar where you fell out of the tree . . . your father's eyes."

But at the same time she was looking at the well-worn black suit and the battered porkpie hat and in her mind I was still the left over, the one who didn't fit or belong, who had always been a convenient whipping boy for Rudy and his brother Theodore, the family scapegoat who took the blame and punishment for everything two cousins did and had to cut out at twelve.

"Where's the clan?" I asked her.

Her eyes darted toward the pair of oak doors that led to the library. "Cat . . . do you think you should . . ."

"Why not, old girl? No hard feelings on my part. What happened is over and I'm not going to be around long enough to get any rumors started. Besides, there's not one thing I want from this bunch of Bannermans. By myself I do okay and no squawks. I'm only passing through."

She was going to say something else, stopped herself and pointed to the doors. "They're all . . . inside there." There was a peculiar edge to her voice, but she was still the family housekeeper and didn't intrude in the closed circle of affairs.

I patted her shoulder, pushed down the two great brass handles and swung the doors open. For one second I had that cold feeling like I used to get when I was told to report and knew what was going to happen. Uncle Miles would be pacing the floor in his whipcord breeches, slapping his leg with the riding crop while he listened to Rudy and Teddy lie about who let the bay mare eat herself to death from the feed bin, or who fired the old cabin out back. I'd know the crop was for me with long hours in the dark attic bedroom and a week of doing backbreaking man-chores to follow until I was allowed the company of the family again. I remembered the way old MacCauley hated to assign the jobs, but he had his orders from Miles and he'd try to take the load off my back, knowing he'd be fired if he was caught. If my old man had been alive he would have knocked his brother's ass off for doing it. But pop had died. He went under a frozen lake to get Rudy who had fallen through, caught pneumonia and a week later was dead.

But it wasn't the same now. Uncle Miles was a skinny, frightened old man who sat behind a desk with a tight face that was all bluster and fear and Rudy and Ted, a couple of pudgy boy-men with faces showing the signs of dissipation and easy living. Neither one of them had much hair left and their faces were pink and soft looking. Ted, who always was the lesser of the two, fidgeted with his hands at a corner of the desk while Rudy stood there pompously with his hands on his hips and his tongue licking his thick lips nervously.

There was a third one I didn't know who was relaxed in a chair with his legs crossed, smoking, an angular guy with thick, black hair and a pointed widow's peak above a face that was strong and handsome.

The other two I did know. One was Carl Matteau, the other Popeye Gage and they were Syndicate boys from Chicago and they both had amused, tolerant expressions on their faces.

Every head in the room swivelled my way when I walked in but there wasn't a sign of recognition on any of them. Miles and his two sons threw a quick look at the pair of hoods, wondering if I were part of them, but when Carl Matteau shrugged they knew I wasn't and Uncle Miles came halfway out of his chair with his face flushed in anger at the intrusion.

"Just what is the meaning of this!" he demanded.

I grinned at him, slow and deliberately. "A social call, Uncle. I came to pay my respects to the family. Relax."

It was Rudy who recognized me first. Something happened to his breath. It seemed to stick in his throat. "Cat he said. "Cat Cay!"

"Hello, Punk." I walked over to him, stood there looking down at his eyes, knowing what he saw scared him stiff. He started to hold out his hand and I slapped him across the mouth.

Teddy never moved for a few moments, then skittered behind the desk. "Are . . . are you crazy?" he managed to get out.

"Sure, kid." I laughed and watched Miles let go the arms of the chair and sink down into the padded seat. He looked even smaller than before.

All he could say was, "*It can't be. It can't be you.*"

But it was and he knew it.

The one sitting behind me, the good looking one, came out of his chair very casually, strode over to the desk and stared at me with eyes as cold as my own. He was as big as I was, but only in height, but he had the kind of build you couldn't trust. A lot of those angular guys could be like whips. "Do you mind explaining who you are?"

I pushed him a little. "You first, buddy."

He rolled with the nudge. "Vance Colby. I happen to be engaged to Anita Bannerman."

Anita! Damn, I had almost forgotten about her. The distant cousin who was ten to my twelve, fair headed and frail who used to follow me around like a puppy. She was another who had sneaked me sandwiches and milk when they had my back against the wall. Cute little kid. She had met me by the gate the night I ran away and kissed me goodbye and ran back to the house crying her eyes out.

"Well, how about that," I said.

"That doesn't explain you."

"I'm a Bannerman, buddy. The bastard Bannerman. You should have heard of me. Max, my old man, and Miles here were brothers. I used to live here."

"So." That was all he said. He nodded as if he knew the whole story and turned to look at Uncle Miles. The old man seemed to be in a stupor.

For some reason the whole thing got funny. Everything was out of focus and there was a charge in the air that you could feel on your skin. I said, "Well, I didn't expect any fatted calf killed for me, but I sure didn't think the clan would be so far on their heels they'd entertain a couple of bums like these two here." I turned around and looked at Matteau and Gage.

It was Gage who started to move until Matteau tapped his arm. "Easy, boy," he said to me.

I walked over to him, gave him one stiff shot in the chops and when he folded I laid one on the back of his neck that piled him into the rug. When Gage reached for the gun I jammed the barrel of the .45 in his mouth and felt teeth snap and saw the blood spill down his chin and the wide eyes of a guy who had just made one hell of a big mistake. He hit the wall, came off it knowing what was going to happen and too late to stop it. I let him have the gunsight across his jaw that laid the flesh open and he went down on top of Matteau with a soft whimper and stayed there.

All you could hear was the terrified silence. It was a noise in itself. I said, "Don't anybody ever call me *boy*," and I looked at the three other Bannermans who never knew any other name for me.

She didn't call me *boy* though. From the doorway where she had seen the whole thing start and end she half whispered, "Cat!"

My love, my little love, only now she wasn't small and frail. Darkly blonde still, but luscious and beautiful with those same deep purple eyes and a mouth that had given me my first kiss. Her breasts accentuated the womanliness of her, dipping into a pert waist and swelling into thighs and calves that were the ultimate in sensuous beauty.

"Hello, Anita," I said.

Even the pair on the floor, the blood or the gun in my fist couldn't stop the headlong rush she made into my arms and hold back the tears. I laughed, grabbed her close a moment and held her back so I could look at her. "I'll be damned," I said, "How you've changed."

Through eyes that were wet and streaking mascara she looked at me. "Cat . . . where did you come from? You were supposed to be dead. Oh, Cat, all these years and you never wrote . . . we never heard a thing. Why didn't . . ."

"I never left anything here, kid." I tilted her chin up with my hand. "Except you. I wanted to take you along but I couldn't have made it then."

"Anita!" Vance Colby was snubbing his cigarette out in an ash tray. He was the only one who seemed calm enough to speak up.

"At ease, friend. We're sort of kissin' cousins. Take it easy until we've said our hellos."

She seemed to see the others then. Like them there was a tension that came back over her, and eyes that were happy, clouded, and her finger bit into my arm. "Please . . . can we go outside . . . and talk?"

I looked at Colby and felt a smile twist my mouth. I put the gun back and said, "Mind?"

"Not at all."

I pointed toward Gage and Matteau. "Better sober up your friends."

CHAPTER TWO

The summer house had always been a place where we could find each other and we went there now. She sat in one of the big wicker chairs and I perched on the railing and said, "Okay, honey, spill it. What's going on here?"

"Cat . . . nothing. Really, I . . ."

"Since when do a pair of hoods sit in the Bannerman mansion? Grandpop or my old man would have thrown them through the nearest window and there was a time when Miles wouldn't let anybody in the front door who wasn't listed in the social register. So what gives, honey?"

"You . . . you knew those two, didn't you?"

"Sure I did. They're Syndicate men they call 'watchers.' They come in while an operation is being set up with Syndicate money to make sure it gets spent right."

"How did you know them?"

"Why?"

"You . . . had a gun."

"So I'm in the same business, that's why, but don't worry about it. What's the score here?"

"I can't tell you," she said simply.

"Swell, so I'll find out myself."

Even in the darkness I could see her hands tighten into hard knots. "Please don't."

"I'm the curious type. Maybe I can stick something up Rudy's tail. He did it to me often enough."

"They're . . . not like they used to be."

"Neither am I, chicken. Now, do you explain?"

"No."

I slid off the rail and stood in front of her. "So tell me and I'll blow," I said. "I don't want anything from those creeps."

Anita shook her head slowly, not wanting to look at me. "I'm afraid, Cat. They did . . . too much to you. Nobody can forget what they did. But please . . . don't make it worse."

"You make it sound interesting." I reached out, lifted her to her feet and put my arms around her. I tried to make it casual, a thing that cousins might do, but it didn't quite work that way. My fingers kneaded the firm structure of her back, my palms pressed her close and some crazy thing went through my head and down through my body and was happening to her too. She said something I couldn't hear because my face was buried in the fragrance of her hair, then my mouth was tasting her and feeling the wild response and fiery dart of her tongue and I had to shove her away with arms that wanted to shake.

"Cat . . . I waited. I never believed what they said . . . about you being dead. The night you left I told you I'd wait."

"We were just kids, honey."

"You said you'd come back for me."

And I remembered. It was why I had turned off the road into the driveway.

"I'm too late, kid."

Her eyes were misty and she leaned her face against my chest. "I know. It can't be changed." She looked up at me. "Take me back, Cat . . . please?"

I left her at the door without bothering to go in. The black Caddie that had been in front of my Ford was gone now, the Buick still there. I got in the car, turned the engine over and drove out the way I had come. Culver City was six miles east and I had nine days before I had to do the job in New York and get back to the coast.

Outside of town I stopped at a second rate motel, put down nine bucks and signed the register. I said I didn't need a receipt, got the key, the guy didn't even bother to look at the name and never commented on it, so I drove down to my room.

After a shower I lay on the bed staring up at the ceiling wondering just how badly I'd like to plaster Rudy and Ted all over their palatial mansion. I laughed at the thought because now it was ridiculous. I could take them both with one hand. I would have settled for a swift kick in the tail or a belt in the puss, dumped old Miles in the cistern out back and called it square.

Except that now a new note was added. The boys from Chicago were on the inside and the fun might be too much to miss out on.

I got up at seven a.m., grabbed breakfast downtown and at eight-thirty when I knew I'd get my party, made a call. Marty Sinclair came on the line with a gruff hello and I said, "Cat Bannerman."

"You in New York?"

"No, Culver City. I'm going to stick around a while."

"You and them crazy broads! When . . ."

"Come on, Marty. I used to live here."

"So why the call?"

"I don't know . . . something cute here we might tie in with. Look, work it easy, but see if you have a line into the local situation."

"Hell, man, Culver City is wide open. Gambling is legal, the horses are out of season but . . ."

"Can you do it?"

"Sure. Take ten minutes."

I gave him the number of the phone booth. "Call me back in fifteen."

He was right on the dot. Fifteen minutes later I knew of a Sid LaMont, had his address and was on the way.

Five sixty one River Street was a sleezy building on the end of a line of apartments with a painted sign advertising a popular beer facing the water. On the ground floor was a printing jobber, a top floor with smashed windows, which put Sidney LaMont right in the middle.

The guy who answered the door was about thirty but looked fifty. He came up to my shoulders, peering at me with a ratty little face, hands fiddling with a dirty undershirt. These guys I knew how to handle without wasting time so I just pushed him back in the room and watched the sweat start forming on his forehead.

They always try a little bull at first. He said, "Look, mister . . . don't you come bustin' in here and . . ."

"Shut up." I didn't have to say any more. When I pulled out the handkerchief and wiped my nose he saw the .45 in the hip holster, swallowed hard and backed into a chair.

"Mac . . . I'm clean, see. I paid my freight. Ask Forbes, he'll tell you. What kind of stuff is this? I'm nickels and dimes. Last week I clear sixty bucks. I don't bother nobody. I . . ."

"Shut up."

I gave him the full treatment, going around the room, just looking until I was satisfied, then pulled up a straight backed chair, turned it around and sat down facing him. His face was wringing wet. So was his undershirt.

"Bannerman," I said. "What do you know about them?"

He seemed genuinely bewildered. *"Them?* Jeez, Mac, I . . ."

"Quick."

The side of his mouth twitched. "You . . . you cops?"

For a full five seconds I just stared at him until his eyes couldn't meet mine at all any more. "I'm not from Culver City," I told him.

Between my face and where the gun was he couldn't keep his eyes still. He said, "So they're big wheels. Live west of here. Hell, I . . ." I started to move my hands and he held up his for me to wait. "Okay, they're real fancy stiffs. You think I meet them? The two kids are always travelling with some hot tomatoes from the clubs and they blow the dough like it's water. The old one's a crap shooter and his brother likes the wheel. So what else do you want? They got the money, let 'em spend it."

I sat without speaking another minute and let him sweat some more, then I got up and walked to the door. I turned around and said, "What do I look like?"

He got the message. "Man, I never seen you in my life."

"Remember that," I said.

There were five major clubs in town all located on the bay side. None of them were open for business, but somebody was in each one and when I told them I was checking on customer credit they weren't a bit backward about obliging me. I mentioned the Bannermans and all I got was a fat okay. They were big spenders and had been for a long time. They paid their bills and could get credit any time they wanted. They weren't big winners, though. Like any habitual players against the house they wound up in the red, but at least they enjoyed the pleasure of laying it out.

But I could still see the gates hanging off their hinges and picture the worn spots in the oriental rug in the library and it didn't make sense. There was just too much pride and tradition behind the Bannermans to let the old homestead run down.

I never knew what the financial set up was. My old man's father had piled up the loot during the gold rush trade. He had made a find, exploited it as far as he could, then sold out to a company. He had split the pile down the middle between Miles and Max, but the old man wasn't one for investments when he could high tail it around the world chasing wine, women and song. Max had me and Miles nursed his dough. And that's how it goes. The snag in the picture was the gaming tables because you can always spend it faster than you can make it and the signs were that the Bannermans weren't what they had been.

I had gone through all the spots where you can usually

pick up a word or two without coming out with a single thing at all. At a quarter to four I tried the public library on State Street, found all the recent issues of the Culver *Sentinel* and started scanning through them.

In two weeks there were five mentions of the Bannermans, all in connection with some civic project or social function, but not a squib about them in the traffic violation column. Three weeks back the headlines were having a ball because there were four rape cases, a hit and run that killed two prominent local citizens, a murder in the parking lot of the *Cherokee Club* and a raid by the Treasury Department men on a narcotics setup in town. The rapes and the narcotics angle were solved, three teen-age kids were being held for the hit and run and the parking lot murder was still up in the air. The dead man there was the lot attendant who had been fooling around with a friend's wife and the husband was being sought after. He was an ex con who had done time for second degree murder and had blown town the night of the killing.

Past that the Bannermans came up again, but only in the society columns. There was one half page of notes and pictures devoted to the engagement of one Anita Bannerman to Vance Colby, a prominent realtor who had settled in Culver City some year and a half before.

When the library closed I went up the hill to Placer Street where the Culver *Sentinel* still turned out the only paper in town and walked in the bar in the next block, sat down and ordered a beer. A few minutes after five-thirty the place started filling up with thirsty types and it wasn't hard to pick out the newshawks in the crowd. But one was a guy I remembered well. He was a little weatherbeaten guy who had lost one ear when he and the old man had sailed the *Turia II* with a load of Canadian booze on board and the Coast Guard hard behind shooting with everything they had. The old man lost the boat and Hank Feathers had lost an ear and I had heard them laugh over the story many a time.

I waited until Feathers squeezed into what seemed to be a customary spot and ordered a drink, then I moved up behind him. I said, "If it isn't Vincent Van Gogh himself."

He put the drink down slowly, craned around and looked at me with the two meanest eyes I ever saw. Old as he was, there was a peculiar stance about him that said he was ready to travel no matter who it was. I grinned at him and the slitted eyes lost some of their meanness.

"That's what you get for sticking your head out a port-hole," I said.

"Damn you, kid, only one man ever knew about that."

"And he liked to call you Van Gogh too didn't he?"

"Okay, son, who are you?"

"The bastard Bannerman. The old man used to tell you lies about my mother."

"Cat Cay! I'll be hanged." His face went into a broad, wrinkled smile and he held out his hand. "Yep, you got his eyes all right. And son, they weren't lies about your mother. I saw her. She was something." He grabbed my arm and pulled me to the bar. "Come on, drink up. Damn if we haven't got something to talk about. What the hell you doing here? I heard you were dead."

"Passing through, that's all."

"See the family?"

"Briefly."

"All slobs. Idle rich and they stink. The girl's okay, but the boys and the old man the world can do without. They got too many people in their pockets."

"Come on, Hank, who could they control?"

He took a pull of the drink and set the glass down. "It's not control exactly, it's just that they've been here long enough to know where the bodies are buried and can play the angles. The old man wants a bit in the paper . . . he gets a bit in the paper. He wants opening night tickets to the Civic Theatre, he gets them. He wants his name out of the paper, he gets that."

"When does he want to be ignored?"

"Ha. Like when Theodore wrapped up two cars in a drunken driving spree and later when his old man had a statutory rape thing squashed for him and like when they interrogated everybody at the *Cherokee Club* after the attendant was killed. But not Rudy. He went home and no mention of him when everybody was listed in black and white. The power of social position, my boy, especially

when wives try to climb the white ladder to the blue book
and politicians need an in through an exclusive club in
the state capital." He stopped and laughed. "But how
about you? Where the hell have you been?"

I shrugged it off. "Ran away at twelve, tied in with a
family of migrant bean pickers until they all died of the
flu, latched on to a rancher in Texas who made sure I
went to school, joined the Army . . . hell, I've been
through the mill."

"You look it, son, you sure do." He cocked his head
then, gave me a kind of sidewise look, his eyes studying
my face intently and he said, "Damn if you don't look familiar. You do anything important?"

"I stayed alive."

"Well, you look familiar."

"I look like the old man, Hank."

He nodded slowly and finished his beer. "Yeah, I guess
that's it, all right. Come on, have another beer."

"No thanks, I have to shove off. Look, I'll see you before I go."

"You better boy, or I'll come after you. Where you
staying?"

I told him the name of the motel, threw some change
on the bar, shook hands and walked out to the Ford.
Things were looking up. The Bannermans weren't as
pure as driven snow after all.

CHAPTER THREE

I had my own contact in Chicago and located Sam
Reed who operated a horse parlor two blocks off The
Loop. I told him to get me a run down on what Matteau
and Gage were doing in Culver City and after the usual
stalling he told me he would. That is, if he could. I wasn't

worried about it. One word to the right people and his tail would be in a sling so he'd be in there pitching to get off the hook.

Then I ate supper and drove back out to the estate.

Annie was like a little bird that night, chirping and flitting around me. She had baked all the goodies I used to like and made me try some of everything before I could get out of the kitchen. Miles, Rudy and Teddy had stayed in town attending to business, but Anita was upstairs in her room.

I tapped on the door, went in when she called and smiled at the lovely doll brushing her hair in front of the mirror. She spun, grinned and opened her arms so I could squeeze her right and said, "I've been waiting to see you all day."

"I've been busy, honey." I held her off and looked at her. "If I knew you were going to turn out like this I never would have left."

It was the wrong thing to say. The smile left her face and those great purple eyes were tinged with that funny sadness again. "Please, Cat."

I nodded. "Okay, kitten, I understand." I let her go.

"Vance has been good to me. It . . . hasn't been easy."

"Sure. But I just don't have to like it."

"I think you'll like him, Cat. He's respectable, dependable . . . and he's done so much."

"Like what?"

She turned back to the mirror, refusing to meet my eyes. "I'd rather not talk about it."

"Fine, honey, one word and no more. Whether he's a nice joe or not in your book, he isn't in mine. Anybody who would tolerate those hoods in this house is scratching me the wrong way. So it's your business and I'm not going to interfere, but something is screwy around here and when I go I'll know about it. What I do about it is another thing."

The brush stopped its motion, then she jerked it through her hair and threw it down on the dressing table. Without looking at me she said, "It isn't like when you left, Cat. They're my family. They're all I have. Please don't do anything."

I switched the subject. "You have a date tonight?"

"No . . . Vance is going to stay in town on business. Some property he's involved with."

"Then suppose we just drop the subject, take in a club, listen to some music, see a show and dance. How about it?"

Her smile was like music. "All right, Cat. I'll be ready in fifteen minutes."

"I'll be downstairs."

But I didn't go downstairs. I went along the balcony to Miles' room and pushed the door open. I took five minutes to shakedown his place and wasted each one. He was a clothes hog, had expensive taste and had nothing tucked away that pointed to trouble.

Teddy's taste was a little more flamboyant. He had a gun rack on the wall with two shotguns, a rifle and six pistols. There must have been a dozen framed pictures of broads placed around, each professional studio shots of the show girl types, each signed with endearing bits of garbage to their wonderful Teddy who had probably kept them in mink coats.

It was Rudy who was the image of his old man. The conservative type who liked the big-business front. I went through his closet, and desk and the dresser drawers, again coming up with the big zero. His bookshelves were lined with the latest novels, predominately historical, and a set of legal tomes, just the thing any clean cut American boy would have around. The only thing out of place was an eight-by-ten photo of a well stacked brunette in a stage bikini and it wasn't signed. The back was tacky with rubber cement and he had probably swiped it from a display somewhere. At least he showed an interest in broads. I put the picture back and went downstairs to wait for Anita.

She was right on time, her dress a simple black thing that seemed to overflow with her, setting the dark blonde of her hair off to perfection. Just watching her come down those stairs made my stomach go hard and for a few seconds I felt all empty inside and cursed myself for having let the years go by. She had waited. *Damn it, she had waited and when I came it was too late!*

"Ready?" she asked me.

"Uh-huh. Where to?"

"Well, you said a club . . ."

"Tonight the best. After that it's peanut butter sandwiches."

"The Cherokee is the best."

"Let's go then."

About five miles northeast the shoreline jutted out into a peninsula an eighth of a mile long. Right at the tip the lights from a low, modern building fanned out into the dock area and batteries of spotlights lit up the parking site. Flanking the roadway on either side all the way in were tennis courts, pitch-'n-putt links and two swimming pools. At the very end a sedate neon sign read, *Cherokee Club*.

Anita said, "How did you know where to go? This has only been up three years."

I didn't tell her I'd been there before checking out the Bannerman credit. "Heard about it in town when I was finding out how much things have changed."

The house was full, and had it not been for Anita I never would even have made the parking lot. Every car there was one of the top three and just as the kid attendant was going to brush me off and catch himself a paste in the mouth, a big guy in a tux came over, saw her and waved the kid away. He threw up a grin and a salute, said, "Sorry, Miss Bannerman, the guy's new here."

"He take the place of the one who got shot?" I said.

"Yeah, and gettin' help ain't easy these days. Punk kids is all you get these days." He stopped and thought a moment. "The other one was knifed, not shot," he added as an afterthought. "Drive up to the door. I'll put your car in Miss Bannerman's usual place."

I slipped the Ford in gear and headed toward the building. "Pretty nice having your own slot. You come here often?"

"Only with Vance. He enjoys the atmosphere."

"He gamble too?"

Anita looked at me sharply, but my face showed nothing. "Very seldom. He's on the conservative side. He prefers investments."

"Good boy."

Inside we got the same preferential treatment from the doorman and headwaiter alike. Before we could be shown to a table a heavyset guy with close-cropped iron gray hair came up smiling, bowed to Anita and gave me a single look wondering where the hell I came from. She introduced him as the owner, Leslie Douglas and when he heard I was another Bannerman the same smile he had for her he gave to me. Old suit or not, if I were a Bannerman I had to be loaded, I guess.

The dining room lay like a horseshoe around a dance floor, butting a stage where an eight piece band played quiet music. There were two bars, one catering only to the men, with the casino area taking up the entire second floor. The layout was professional. Not the loose Vegas or Reno attitude that would take anybody's nickel, but more on the Monte Carlo style, catering to a single class. Big Money. I felt as much at home as a cat in a dog kennel.

For two hours we drank, talked and danced. For two hours we were those kids again laughing about the things that had happened because now they were pathetically funny. For two hours I lied to her about all those years in between then and now because I didn't want her to know. And for two hours we were in love like nothing before and we knew it.

But there was nothing we could do about it. She had the Bannerman pride of honesty and I had the sense to keep my mouth shut even though I felt like exploding.

At five minutes to midnight she excused herself to go to the powder room and I waved for another drink. Before it came I saw the big guy edging over to my table, smiling and talking to the others on the way until he reached me. His nose had been broken, he had one twisted ear and under his clothes you knew there were great chunks of muscle that could hurt you bad if he wanted to.

He nodded at an empty chair and said, "Mind?"

"No, sit down. Want a drink!"

"Thanks. I'm on duty."

"Bouncing?"

His shoulders moved in a massive shrug. "It ain't really necessary. I just speak to 'em generally."

"That's the only way."

The guy was getting to something. He waited until I had the drink and leaned back languidly. "You got a rod on you, ain't you?"

"Sure," I said, "but it ain't really necessary. I just speak to 'em generally."

The frown broke into a hoarse laugh and he shook his head. "Like my kid says, you're cool, man."

"Got to be in this business."

"Ain't why I came though. Les told me you was a Bannerman. That right?"

"Sad, but true."

"Couldn't be old Cat Cay Bannerman, could it?"

I looked at him, trying to get his point. I nodded.

"Maybe you don't remember me. I got my face busted up in the ring, but I was different when I was a kid. Petey Salvo's the name. We went to the Ringdale school together."

I let out a laugh and stuck out my hand. "I'll be damned," I said. "Woppo Salvo, the kid who got his head stuck in the fence posts."

"You remember that?" he grinned.

"Hell, yes, like I remember the times you and me had it out in the lots for something or other. It's been a long time."

"Too long." He let his eyes go over my face. "You do some fighting?"

"Some."

"You look it. Stupid racket. How long you gonna be around?"

"Few days, maybe."

"Suppose we get together some time? Plenty things changed around here. You want to meet anybody, let me know."

"Good idea."

Petey Salvo shuffled the chair back and got ready to leave. "When I first saw you come in here I thought I recognized you from somewhere. Guys I get to know are the ones shouldn't be here so I was gonna heave you until

Les give me the nod. Then I figured you was like a body-guard to Miss Bannerman."

"She need one?"

"Her? Hell, she's the only decent one. It's those kids who are bums. The night Chuck Maloney got knifed and everyone got questioned he paid off to get hustled out of here and didn't even get his name in the papers."

I picked up my glass. "Maybe he stuck him."

"Yeah, that'll be the day. Maloney was an ex-marine and had thirty-one fights in the ring and when that powderpuff can close in on him I'll eat his shoes. He's strictly yellow, you know that. I saw a dame beat the hell out of him one night." He stood up and held out his hand again. "I'm around all the time. Look me up."

"Sure will, Petey."

"Stay for the next show. Real specialty number. Chuck Maloney's wife is doing a strip. Les gave her the job to kinda help things along for her. She used to do a circuit in the east and swings pretty good."

"I'll catch it."

Anita came back then, saw Petey leaving and said, "Company?"

"We used to go to school together, Ringdale P. S. where the Bannermans joined the *hoi polloi* to have the democratic flavor infused into their veins."

The lights dimmed then and a spot hit the dance floor. From the band came a sharp chord that was sustained until the M.C. came out with a hand mike and got everyone's attention. His announcement was brief . . . the Cherokee Club was about to offer its feature attraction for the evening, a blazing redhead who had set fire to stages all over the country and was persuaded to visit the club for a two week showing. And introducing, Irish Maloney and her drumbeat rhythm!

The bongos and the base started their beat, were joined by a single clarinet and out of the wings came the redhead. She was good, no doubt about that. She had crazy muscular control of every part of her body and could start a ripple going in her thighs that worked its way up her belly to her breasts and undulate back down again. She stayed there working the perimeter of the floor with her body inches away from gaping eyes for a full half hour until the drums gave out and she ran off in a wild burst of applause from everyone in the room.

She was interesting, all right . . . but the most interesting part was that she was the same doll whose picture I had seen in Rudy's room, only then the red hair had photographed brunette.

Anita said, "She was beautiful, wasn't she?"

"I like you better. Ready to go?"

"Whenever you are."

I paid the tab, got her coat for her, said good night to Leslie Douglas on the way out and picked up the Ford myself. The kid in charge didn't seem anxious to tool anything less than a Caddie.

At the house I walked her to the door, turned her around and said, "Thanks for the night, honey."

She was crying. "Cat . . ."

"Look, I know. I know the reasons and the answers."

"Why does it have to be like this?"

"Because there's no other way. At least you're a real Bannerman. I'm still the bastard, remember."

"Please don't say that."

"Why fight the truth? There are two ends to the family . . . stay with the big one."

There was a funny light in her eyes when she said it. "I may at that."

Petey Salvo came out at three-thirty when the casino was empty. We drove a couple of miles to a drive in, ordered hamburgers and coffee and after a few minutes of old times I got to the point. "Petey . . . what's with this Maloney dish?"

"Ah, come on Cat, lay off her. She gave Chuck enough trouble. You don't want none of it."

"Who says I do?"

"Well, more guys get a stiff one for that broad than any I ever saw. She was always runnin' and Chuck was always belting some punk who went after her. She drove him nuts."

"Look . . . what about that guy the cops are after?"

"Him . . . Sanders? So he tried making a play for her

and Chuck nailed him. He did it a couple more times and Chuck did the same thing. But the broad kept the guy coming back. She liked to see the action, that's what I think. Chuck should never've taken her out of show biz. He was better off without her."

"Rudy Bannerman."

"What about him?"

"He ever try for any of that?"

Petey bit into a hamburger and scowled. "You crazy? Chuck would've mangled him."

"So did he?"

"Ah, everybody tried one time or another. She used to hang around the tables a lot and you know how it goes. That Rudy makes like he's a wheel to all the dames and feels good when they play up to him, but he knew what would happen. Anyway, he's a damn drunk."

"So?"

"So when he gets loaded he's no good. I heard a couple of the kids he had out laughing about the guy. He's . . . he's . . . what's the word?"

"Impotent?"

"Yeah. No balls. Nothin' much else either. The dames laugh at him. Big guy and he falls apart in bed and bawls." He finished the other hamburger and washed it down with the coffee. "What you getting to anyway?"

"A little matter of blackmail, I think. I'm beginning to get ideas about how Maloney was killed."

"Well, if you find out, let me know first. Him and me were buddies."

CHAPTER FOUR

The first thing in the morning I called through to Chicago and got Sam Reed. In a hushed voice that always sounded scared when he was passing out a line he told me he had checked through on Popeye Gage and

Carl Matteau and found out they were sent to Culver City ten days ago along with a bagman carrying a hundred grand that was going to set up an operation. The bagman came back, Gage and Matteau stayed to make sure Syndicate dough was spent like it was supposed to be. The only odd note was that although Popeye Gage was one of the "watchers," Matteau had come up in the organization the last few years and didn't take assignments like this unless he had a going interest in things. The word was that whatever the operation was to be, Matteau would run it. He was overseeing his product personally. The other bit was that Popeye had become a junkie and was pretty damn dangerous.

I told Sam thanks, said I'd return the favor and gave him the name of my motel in case anything else came up. He told me he would and broke the connection. Ordinarily Sam was close mouthed and it hurt him to get squeezed.

After breakfast I found out where Hank Feathers lived, got him out of the sack cussing up a storm until he knew it was me, then got invited over for coffee.

Hank lived alone in a small house outside of town. The old man and he used to laugh about their escapades with the women, but Hank never seemed to stick to one long enough to make it permanent. The place was small enough for him to take care of and served as a second office when necessary, and offered all the comforts a bachelor type could need.

When we got settled I said, "You did the story the night Maloney got killed at the Cherokee, didn't you?"

"Yeah, two columns. There wasn't anything to say."

"Run through it, will you?"

He watched me over the coffee cup. "Damn if you aren't your old man all over again. Get a nut in your head and you can't shake it loose."

"Well?"

Hank put the cup down and spread his hands. "Nothing. The guy was lying there dead with a knife hole in his chest. No scuffle, no nothing."

"Motive?"

"He had a five hundred buck watch some drunken clown gave him and a hundred eighty some odd bucks in his pocket. It wasn't robbery. He must have known the guy and didn't expect a shiv."

"Could have been something else."

"Oh?"

"Maybe he just wasn't afraid of him. He didn't expect the knife, but he wasn't scared."

"The cops had that angle too." He sipped his coffee again. "Not me though. I'd say it came as a complete surprise."

"Why?"

"He had a pack of club matches in one hand. There was a single unstruck match lying near the body. I'd say he was going to light a cigarette for somebody he knew when he got it in under the arms."

"The police reach the same conclusion?"

"Nope. Where he was were a lot of butts and some loose ones that fell out of his pocket. He always carried them loose. They say he was going to light his own and the guy caught him in that position."

I nodded, thought it through and finished my coffee. "I'd like a list of people who were there that night."

"Sure, check out two hundred reputable citizens and see what you can find. I tried it. What are you after anyway?"

"Something named Bannerman," I said. "Rudy Bannerman."

Hank Feathers grinned and leaned back into the chair. "Why didn't you ask it? He was plastered. He had just dropped fifteen G's in the casino and got loaded at the bar. When the cops came they found him in the men's room locked in a toilet sick as a pig. He had puked his ears off and sobered up pretty fast . . . enough to get himself out of there in a hurry, but he couldn't have raised a burp far less than a knife."

"The cops ever find the weapon?" I asked him.

"Not likely. The police surgeon said it was made by a stiletto with a six inch blade three quarters of an inch wide at the base. With all the water around here to throw it into there's little chance of finding it. Whoever killed him had plenty of time to dump the knife . . . Maloney was dead twenty minutes before anybody knew about it."

"Nicely set up."

"Wasn't it though? Now you got something on your mind, boy. Get with it. I'll feed you, but let's you feed me too."

"Feel up to stepping on toes?"

"Son, that's my life."

"Okay, see if Irish Maloney ever had anything to do with Rudy Bannerman."

"Brother!"

"He had a picture of her in his room. Care to try it!"

"You just bought it, son. I hope you don't get hurt."

"I've been hurt all I'll ever be, Hank."

The Bannerman name carried a lot of weight. There was only one family of them in Culver City and whoever bore it was set apart as a special person to be considered in a unique fashion. And like all families who occupied that niche, little was unknown about them no matter what it was. From the docks to the country clubs, they knew my old man and liked him, but the rest were another breed entirely.

They knew about the bastard Bannerman too, but as long as he was part of old Max he was right and it was the in I needed. It hadn't taken long for word to get around once I planted the seed. All they wanted to know was that I was a Bannerman and I had plans.

I hit three of the largest realtors, sat through cocktails twice and a lunch and came up with a talker when I found Simon Helm and got the idea across that I was back looking to establish a moderate smokeless industry somewhere in the area. After a few drinks he showed me the maps, pointed out suitable locations, let me digest his thoughts and settled down to the general discussions that precede any deal.

Vance Colby's name had to come up. Helm asked me bluntly why I didn't go through my prospective cousin-in-law to make a buy and just as bluntly I said I didn't like him.

"Well," Helm said, "I'm afraid a lot of us share your opinion." He let out a short laugh. "Not that he's greedy or crooked . . . I'm afraid he's a little too shrewd for us country folks. For the little while he's been here he's made some big deals."

"It figures."

"Now he's got the property adjacent to the new city marina. You know what that means?"

"Prime land," I said.

"Even better. If anyone puts up a club there the expense of a water landing is saved, it's cheap filled property in the best spot around with the advantage of having access to all major highways."

"That's an expensive project."

"His commission will be enormous. It would be better still if he did it himself."

"That's a multi-million dollar project."

"It can be financed," he said.

"Is he that big?"

"No," Simon Helm said slyly, "but with Bannerman money behind him it could be done. Quite a coup."

"I'll take it the hard way."

He nodded energetically. "I don't blame you. Now, when would you like to look at the properties?"

"In a day or two. I have them spotted and I'll drive out myself. If I make a decision I'll contact you."

"A pleasure, Mr. Bannerman. I'm happy you came to me."

"So am I, Mr. Helm."

Right after supper I called Petey Salvo and asked him if he could stop by my motel before he went to the club. He said he'd be there by eight and didn't ask any questions. I drove back, had a hot shower, shaved and took out the .45 and went through the ritual of cleaning it, then laid it on the table while I pulled on my clothes.

It was just seven forty-five when the knock came on my door and I opened it hanging onto my pants, figuring Petey was early.

This time I figured wrong. The two of them came in easy with Popeye Gage levelling a snub nosed Banker's Special at my gut and his eyes lit up like a neon sign. Behind him was Carl Matteau and the smile he wore was one of total pleasure because this kind of business was his kind of business and he enjoyed every minute of it.

"Back," he said. "Real quiet, guy."

I wasn't about to argue with the gun. All I could do

was toss the towel I had in my hand on the table to cover up the .45 laying there and hope they didn't catch the act. That much I got away with if it could do any good. The only other thing I could do was pull the scared act and button up my pants just to be doing anything and Popeye Gage grinned through his swollen mouth and let me have the side of the gun across the temple.

Before he moved I saw it coming and rolled enough to miss most of it, but it slammed me back against the bed and I hit the floor face down. Matteau said, "More, Popeye."

He worked me hard then, his feet catching my ribs and my arms, but only once did he land one on my head and then he nearly tore my scalp off. He was laughing and sucking air hard to get the boot into me and every time he did all I could think of was how hard I was going to step on his face when my time came. He stopped for a few seconds and I made the mistake of turning my head. When I did the butt end of the gun smashed down on the back of my skull like a sledge hammer and I felt my chin and mouth bite into the floor and the ebb and flow of unconsciousness that never quite came. All I had was that terrible pounding inside my brain and the complete inability to move any part of my body.

But Carl knew when I was all there again. He said, "Talk up, wise guy."

"Should I make him?" Popeye said.

"No, he'll do it himself."

I dragged myself away from the bed, tried to sit up and tasted the salty taste of blood in my mouth.

"Nobody pulls the kind of crap you did and gets away with it," Carl told me slowly. "Now let's hear it."

I shook my head. I couldn't get any words out.

"You don't belong here. Why, punk?"

"I . . . lived here."

"Sure. So why'd you come back?"

"Vacation. I was . . . going east."

"Let me . . ."

"Shut up, Popeye. This guy's a punk. Look at him. Take a look at his face, all beat up. He packs a rod, he's got nothing behind him so he's a punk. He comes back to put the bite on the family like any punk will do only now he gets no bite. He gets wise with me and he gets nothing except his face all smashed in or a bullet in his belly if he tries to play it smart. See his car? Six years old. You checked his duds . . . all junk. Someplace he's a small time punk, a cheap hood and these mugs we deal with the same old way, right, Bannerman?"

"Look . . ."

It was almost time for Petey to show. I hoped he'd know how to play it.

"Out," Matteau said. "Tonight you leave. You stay one more day and you get buried here."

I was going to tell him to drop dead when he nodded to Popeye Gage and the gun came down again. This time there was no intermediate darkness. It was all nice and black and peaceful and didn't hurt a bit until I woke up.

And that was when Petey Salvo was shaking me. He was twenty minutes late. I was half naked and he was slopping off the blood and holding a wet towel to the cut on my head making noises like the second in the corner of a losing fighter.

I said, "Hi, Petey."

"What the hell happened to you? The door was open so I came in thinkin' you was sacked out and you're all over blood. You have a party going?"

I sat up, got to my feet and squatted on the edge of the bed. "Yeah, I had a surprise party from a couple of goons."

"Then come on, man, we'll nail 'em. You know who they were?"

"I know."

"So where do we go?"

"No place, pal."

He took the towel away and looked at me, his face puzzled. "You just gonna take it like that?"

I shook my head and it hurt. "No."

"So let's go then."

I pushed his hand away. "Let it be, buddy. I've had the treatment before. It proves a point right now and when the time comes I'll lay those pigs out all the way."

"How come you got took?"

"I thought it was you."

"Shit." He seemed embarrassed. "If I didn't get inna argument with the old lady I coulda been here."

"Forget it. In a way I'm glad it happened. The guys who took me should have knocked me off. Only now they hand me walking papers and expect me to move out." I looked up at the huge hulk of the guy and grinned. "They got the wrong Bannerman. I'm the bastard, remember?"

"Hell, I know you ain't chicken. I just don't like that stuff. Why you take it anyway?"

"Because it ties in with Maloney's murder, kid. I want the one who did it and why. So stop sweating. This Cat got nine lives."

"Sure. How many did you use up already?"

"About seven," I said.

It took another scalding hot shower and a bruising rubdown by Petey to get me back in shape, but when it was over all I had was a small headache and a bunch of bruises. Then we got in the two cars and he did what I asked him to do.

He took me over to see Irish Maloney to introduce me as an old buddy who heard his friend was dead and came by to pay his respects to the widow.

It was a small house with a small garden and a two year old car in the garage halfway down Center Drive. It wasn't much, but all the signs were there of a guy who tried to make the best of what he had in every way and I knew what Chuck Maloney really felt about his wife.

On the stage she was sensational, but meeting her stretched out on a chaise under a sun lamp was another thing. Oh, she had the lumps in the right places, the hippy curves and the full breasts that modern culture demands, the sensuous look that comes from Max Factor tins, but there were other things that took her down all the way. Clever lighting could take years off her, but up close you could see the years closing in, the tiny wrinkles around the eyes and the beginning of the flesh getting slack and the striations on the upper parts of her thighs where the skin had stretched sometime when she ate her way out of the burlecue circuit.

Yet inside her mind she was still twenty years old and all men were at her feet and she was able to prove it

nightly at the Cherokee and forget that sheer profession-
alism and the help of electricians could put her across.

Petey said, "This here's my friend, Cat." He looked at
me and conveniently forgot my last name. "Cat Cay. He
was Chuck's friend too. He just wanted to talk, so I'll
leave you guys alone. I got to get to the club. You got
another hour yet, Irish."

I got the full treatment when Petey left; the way she sat
up, took off the sun glasses and doubled her legs under
her to make sure I got the full benefit of everything she
had to show. The shorts were tight and showed the voluptuous V of her belly and deliberately low enough to show
where she had shaved to fit into her costume. She leaned
over to make me a drink from the decanter on the table,
curving herself so I would be impressed by the way the
halter held her breasts high and firm, pushing out over
the top so the nipples were almost exposed.

Too many times I had gone the route before and knew
the action so I could afford to ignore the invitation and
when I took the drink and sat down opposite her I let her
see my eyes and read my face until she knew I was what
I was, but couldn't quite understand it.

I said, "Sorry about Chuck. He was a good friend. We
were in the Marines together."

She lifted her glass, toasted me with a silent kiss.
"That's how it goes."

"No remorse?"

"He was a little man."

"I don't know."

"He got himself killed, didn't he? This guy
Sanders . . ."

She didn't let me finish. "Sanders was a nothing too.
He couldn't kill a fly. All he was scared of was being put
back in the pen." Irish Maloney downed the drink in
three fast gulps and set the glass down.

"He wasn't a Rudy Bannerman?"

"Who?"

"Rudy."

"Him?" she said, "A nothing. Strictly nothing. A boy
in long pants. He's good for a goose when nobody's watch-

ing and nothing more." She smiled at me, loose and wanting. "What kind of man are you, Mr. Cay?"

"Big," I said.

"Not if you were Chuck's friend. He never had big friends."

"In the Marines he had."

"Then come here and show me." ·

She reached her hand down and a zipper made that funny sound and the shorts were suddenly hanging loose down one side. She smiled again, her mouth wet and waiting and she leaned back watching me.

I stood up. "Thanks for the offer, honey, but like I said, Chuck was my friend. There should be a period of mourning."

I thought she'd get mad. They usually do, but not her. She giggled, blinked her eyes and made a mouth at me. "Ohoo, you *got* to be a big man to say no."

"Not necessarily."

The giggle again. Then she hooked her thumbs in the hem of the shorts, stripped them off in one swift motion, held them high overhead and let them fall to the floor. She let herself fall back into the chaise-longue in a classic position, still smiling, knowing damn well what was happening to me. *"Now say no."* Her voice was husky with the beat in it.

"No," I said.

I walked to the door, opened it and turned around. She hadn't changed position or stopped smiling. Before I could find the right words Irish Maloney said, "I'm coming to get you, big man."

"I'm not hard to find," I told her.

When I was in the Ford and on the way back to town I knew one thing. I had found a good motive for murder. The thing was, how did it tie in with Gage and Matteau being involved with the Bannermans? There was one way to find out.

CHAPTER FIVE

I walked around the house and went in the back way where Annie was cleaning up in the kitchen. When I tapped on the door her head jerked up, birdlike, and she put the tray of dirty glasses in the sink and minced to the porch, flicked the light on and peered out into the dark. "Yes . . . who is it?"

"Cat, honey. Open up."

She smiled happily, pulled the latch and I stepped inside. "My word, boy, what are you doing coming in the backway? You *are* a Bannerman."

"Hell, Annie, it's the only way I was ever allowed in the house anyway. You forget?"

"Well you don't have to do that now."

"This time I did," I said. "I want to talk to you before I see them."

Her mouth seemed to tighten up and she half turned away. "If you don't mind . . . I'm . . . only an employee. Please . . ."

"In the pig's neck. You were the only old lady I ever had. If it hadn't been for you and Anita they would have starved me out long before I left. The Bannermans don't have room for a bastard in their great halls of luxury." I put my arm around her and led the way to the breakfast niche and sat down opposite her.

"Look, honey. Nothing goes on around here that you don't know. You have eyes like an eagle and ears like a rabbit and there isn't a keyhole or pinprick in a wall you haven't peeked through. Any secrets this family have, you have too, even if you do keep them locked behind sealed lips. That's well appreciated if it's for the good, but right

156

now something is wrong and there's big trouble going on . . ."

"You . . . can only make it worse."

"Do you know about it?"

She hesitated, then her eyes dropped in front of my gaze. "Yes," she said simply.

"So what's the pitch."

"I . . . don't think I should tell you."

"I can find out the hard way, Annie. The trouble might get worse then."

She fidgeted with the salt shaker on the table a moment, then looked up. "It's Rudy," she said. "He killed the attendant at the Cherokee Club."

"What?"

She nodded. "It's true. He was drunk and he gets mean when he's drunk and doesn't get his own way. He . . . went to get his car and the attendant thought he had too much to drink to drive and wouldn't get the car and Rudy . . . went back inside . . . and got the knife . . . and stabbed him."

I reached over and grabbed the fragile hand. "Who says so, Annie?"

"Those two men . . . they were there. They had just driven up."

The picture began to form then. "So they picked up the knife after Rudy ran for it and they got the thing with his fingerprints all over it," I stated.

"Yes."

"What does Rudy say about it?"

She shook her head sadly. "He doesn't remember a thing. He was drunk and sick. He can't remember anything."

"And now they want money, is that it?"

"Yes . . . I think so. I . . . really don't know."

"Everybody inside?"

"They're waiting for Vance. Yes, they're inside."

I got up, gave her hand a squeeze and told her not to worry. Then I went out the kitchen, through the hall into the library where the clan was gathered looking like they were waiting for a bomb to hit.

From the expression on their faces, when they saw me,

they saw the bomb coming. Old Uncle Miles grabbed the arms of the chair and his face turned white. Rudy, who had been pacing the floor with his hands behind his back, suddenly became too flaccid to stand and tried to look nonchalant as he settled on the arm of the chair Teddy was cowering in.

Only Anita seemed genuinely glad to see me, her smile erasing the worry look as she left the couch to come across the room with her hand out. I knew what she was thinking, all right; she could steer me out of there before I churned things up. But even she wasn't going to stop what I was going to do.

I hooked my arm under hers and went to the desk where Miles was glowering at me and sat on the edge. Everybody had something to say, but nobody wanted to speak. I looked at chubby cousin Rudy and said, "Hear you're sweating a murder charge, cousin."

That was the bomb going off. You could hear the hiss of breath, the sucking sounds, the sudden jerking movements as the words hit them. All Anita did was tighten her hand on mine and look down at the floor.

"How . . . did you find out?"

Over my shoulder I said, "Easy, Uncle. I just asked around. I saw Gage and Matteau here and put two and two together. To me they add up. Dear cousin Rudy's got his ass in a sling he can't get out of and it's about time it happened. I'm happy for one thing though . . . I'm here to see it. And it doesn't only hit the fat slob, it breaks down to Teddy and you too, Miles. You'll never hold your heads up around here again. From now on you'll be the joke of the community and when they strap old killer Rudy there in the chair the Bannerman family comes to a screaming halt."

Rudy looked like he'd get sick. Miles kept swallowing hard, his scrawny chest gulping air.

"And me, Cat?" Anita asked.

"You're going to be a Colby, honey. You won't be wearing the Bannerman name."

"Do you think he'll have me?"

"Does he know about this?"

"Yes, he does. He's helping all he can."

"How?"

She glanced at Miles, wondering whether to tell me or not, then made the decision for herself. "He's tried to make a settlement with those men. He's threatened them and everything else, but they can't be moved. They . . . want an awful lot of money."

"How much?"

Rudy broke in, his voice weak. "See here, Anita . . ."

"Shut up, Rudy," I said. He did, and fast. "Go on, Anita."

"A . . . million dollars."

I let out a soft, slow whistle. "Well, it looks like Rudy's making a real dent in the family budget. What are you going to do about it?"

They all tried to look at each other at once. I caught the exchange and grinned at them. Finally Miles croaked, "We'll see that . . . it is paid, not that it is any of your affair."

"And what happens?" I slid off the desk, turned around and leaned on it and faced Miles down. "Rudy gets off the hook and the Sanders guy eventually gets nailed by the cops. He's got a prison record and a possible motive for killing Maloney. He's got no alibi and he loused things up by taking off when he heard of the killing. There's no murder weapon for evidence and the jury thinks it has a solid case and gives him the black verdict and the guy gets the chair. How are the Bannermans going to feel then when they know one of their own is responsible for the death of two people now and the real killer is inside their own house?"

Rudy did get sick then. He let out a soft moan, grabbed his stomach and ran from the room.

Miles said, "What are you . . . thinking of?"

I straightened up and glanced around the room. "I don't know. I sure got an ax over your heads now. You beat me to the ground when I wasn't old enough to fight back and now I might have some fun."

"*Oh, Cat . . . .*" Anita's eyes were bright with tears. She looked at Miles first, then Teddy and at Rudy who came back with a face as white as snow. "Don't do that to them . . . they're such . . . such nothings anyway."

I nodded, "Don't feel sorry for them sugar, maybe I

can instill some character in them. Maybe Rudy will get an urge of integrity and decide to come clean."

One look at Rudy made that a joke. Rudy wasn't going to confess to anything.

I had something else to tell them they would like to have heard, but the entrance of Vance Colby stopped that. He strode into the library as if it were his own, immediately sensed the situation and said directly to Anita in an accusing tone. "You told him."

She let go my arm. "He found out by himself."

"And may I ask what this matter has to do with you?"

"If you're looking for a smack in the chops you're going about it the right way, buddy."

His smile was hard and the curious glint in his eyes painted the picture nicely. The casual way he walked up didn't hide the sudden bunching of muscles under his coat. He said, "Am I?"

And before he could start the judo chop I belted him in the damn mouth so hard the skin of my knuckles split on his teeth and he rolled twice before the couch stopped him and he looked up at me with a face full of hate as big as your hat. He was one of those over-confident types who had put in too many hours in a gym wearing a Jap toga and practicing un-American fighting and he forgot about a straight right to the kisser. Hell, I'd had it out with dozens of these types before. "The next time I may shoot you, Vance."

I pushed my coat back to get at a handkerchief for my hand and let him see the .45. He didn't answer. He kept both hands to his mouth and tried to sit up.

"Aren't you going to help him, Anita?"

"No," she said solemnly, "I knew what he was going to do. I've seen him do it before. I think Vance needed that lesson. He can get up by himself."

Very gently, I leaned down and kissed the top of her head. "Thanks, kitten." I took her arm and started out the library. At the front door I said, "Look, I'd sooner see them sweat than start trouble, but don't you get involved in this mess. That Maloney kill is still wide open and there's no statute of limitations on murder. There's something fishy going on here and I'm going to dig it out. I want you to do me a favor."

"What, Cat?"

"Let me know what they plan to do. Everything, okay?"

"Okay, darling." She frowned at what she said, then smiled softly. She reached up and touched my face. "I can trust you."

"You won't get hurt," I told her. I kissed her mouth and the tip of her nose, but it wasn't enough. She was back there in my arms again for one fierce moment and it was us, just us and no one else. I knew my fingers were hurting her arms and I pushed her away feeling my heart smashing against my ribs.

"We'll make it, baby."

"No . . . we never can. I wish . . . but we can't."

I left her like that and went out to the car. At any time now the stuff was going to hit the fan.

At the motel I told the clerk at the desk I'd be around a little while yet, paid the bill up to date and went to my room. I double locked the door, shoved the .45 under my pillow, showered and flaked out with the radio playing softly in my ear.

Popeye Gage and Carl Matteau. They came to town behind a bagman who carried a hundred grand and it could be it was to set up an operation for Matteau. Luck played into their hands when they saw Maloney killed and picked up the evidence. His original investment had now increased tenfold if he pulled it off.

I reached to switch the radio off when the late news came on from the local station and the first item the announcer read off was that Guy Sanders, prime suspect in the Chuck Maloney murder, had been picked up in Seattle, Washington and arrangements were being made for his extradition.

CHAPTER SIX

The morning papers had it all laid out. There was a full statement from the D.A. who claimed there was no doubt concerning Sanders's guilt and felt certain a confession could be obtained after an interrogation. He rehashed the details of the crime and stated that Sanders would be brought to trial as soon as feasible.

On the inside pages an editorial went through it again, crying out the need for justice and lauding the D.A. for his attitude concerning the affair. It looked like Sanders had had it. As far as the city was concerned, the investigation was over. Only the prosecution remained.

After I got dressed and ate I drove around for two hours checking out the properties Simon Helm had suggested to me, jotting down quick notes so I could have an intelligent though phoney conversation with him. When I finished it was a little after ten a.m. and I got to his office just as he was coming in.

For the kind of deal he was hoping to set up with me he was willing to forego all other engagements and took me back into his office with orders to his secretary not to disturb us. She had coffee ready, set us up and left.

"Now, Mr. Bannerman, how did you like the sites I pointed out?"

"Only two have possibilities," I said. "The old Witworth estate and the Flagler Hill section. However, they both lack one essential . . . a water table sufficient to my needs."

"How would you know about that?" he asked with a degree of surprise.

"When you know how to ask questions you get some great answers. It's my business."

"Well, I heard this rumor, but never gave it a thought. My, we have to find something else quickly."

"I'll tell you what I have in mind."

"Oh?"

"You'll have to investigate the deal . . . but it'll all be a matter of public record anyway. Check out that property my future cousin-in-law has next to the proposed city marina."

"But Mr. Bannerman . . ."

"For my purposes it's ideal. The building will be modern, handsome, the industry smokeless, the access highways are at hand . . . a railroad siding can be extended from the Tompson works and the benefits to the city will be far greater than that of another gambling casino."

"But . . ."

"No buts, Mr. Helm. If you don't want to handle it there are others."

He couldn't fight that attitude. He shrugged and drank his coffee. "Very well, I'll see how far things have gone. However, if it is not possible . . ."

"Then I'll have to take something else," I finished for him. "How long will it take?"

He glanced at the clock on the wall. "If I get to it right away . . . perhaps this afternoon."

I got up and reached for my hat. "I'll be back later."

"Certainly, Mr. Bannerman," he said, rolling his tongue around the name.

Hank Feathers didn't reach his office until a little before noon. I whistled out the window of the car and he came plodding across the street all grin and crinkly eyes and got in beside me.

"Step on any toes?" I asked him.

"Well now, son, I don't know yet. I got up around the Maloney place and funny enough I know quite a few people up there. One of our printers has a place two houses away and a garrulous wife. Anyway, after due poking around I came up with a lot of answers."

"Gossip or answers?"

"You do the separating," Hank said. "This Maloney woman has quite a neighborhood reputation. She made no bones about her conduct, rather enjoying the Madame Pompadour concept. She had plenty of visitors, plenty."

"Anybody special?"

"Don't jump the gun, son," he smiled, holding up his hands. "Rudy Bannerman was positively identified having tried to gain admittance on two occasions, both times while he was crocked. One, during an afternoon, he was seen for better than an hour in her back yard while she was sunbathing. The whole thing was observed and though he was well tempted by that lovely dish, he stoutheartedly left before the husband returned."

"Good for him."

"The suspect Guy Sanders made several surreptitious trips to visit Irish and twice was seen with her in a neighborhood bar. It's enough to hang him."

"They'll sure try it."

"But here's the interesting note. From a couple of very nosey sources, one an old lady given to staying up late and the other our printer's wife who has some odd habits including insomnia, I learn that there was one fairly common visitor to the Maloney household when the husband was on the late shift at the Cherokee Club."

"Any description?"

"Very little. He was always dressed in a suit or topcoat, wore a hat and moved fast. Generally he drove up, apparently at a specified time and she came out, joined him in the car and they drove away."

"Car?"

"What old dame can identify a new car at night? It was a dark one, that's all. They suspect that he was Sanders."

"Great. What do you think?"

Hank shrugged, looked at me and said, "The guy was thin . . . so is Sanders. Rudy Bannerman is chubby. At least it wasn't him. Anything else you want me to get in trouble over?"

"I'll think of something."

He opened the door and stepped out, then remembered something and said, "By the way, I bumped into a guy who wants to see you very badly. A friend of your old man's."

"Who?"

"George P. Wilkenson, the family solicitor."

"Wilkenson? Damn, he must be ninety years old."

"Ninety-three. He's still active. Anyway, I told him you were back and he said it was urgent you get up and see him. He lives back in the past these days and can still chew your ears off. He and your old man were great fishing buddies."

"I'll say hello before I leave," I said. "And hey . . . who's a cop you can trust? Somebody with a gold badge."

"Try Lieutenant Travers. Tell him I recommended him."

I waved so-long, drove back downtown and cut over to the Municipal Building that housed the First Precinct and went in and asked for Lieutenant Travers. The desk sergeant made the call, told me to go on back and gave me directions.

Travers was pretty young as Lieutenants go, but he had all the little earmarks that stamped him as a professional law enforcement officer. Tough when he had to be, smart always, cute when necessary and suspicious eternally. He gave me one of those long slow up-and-down looks when I walked in, was ready enough with a handshake and an invitation to sit down and had I not left the .45 and the speed rig in the car he would have spotted it and shaken me down on the spot. He caught the name, but it didn't cut any ice with him at all.

"Related to the Bannerman family locally?" He held out a pack of butts and I shook my head.

"In a way. I'm a bastard." His eyes jumped up. "A real one . . . born out of wedlock and all that crap."

He sucked on his cigarette. "Yeah, I've heard that story. Now, what can I do for you?"

"I've recognized two Chicago hoodlums in this town, Lieutenant. One is Popeye Gage and the other Carl Matteau."

Travers watched me, swung slowly in his chair a few times and said, "I know they're here, but how did *you* recognize them, Mr. Bannerman?"

I had to grin. "Got in a little deal in Chicago once and they were pointed out as Syndicate men. They both have records and I thought you might like to know about it."

"Uh-huh." He took another big drag on the butt and laid it down. "We appreciate your being civic minded, but there's nothing we can do. Is there a complaint you'd like to lodge?"

"Nope, but since I'm considering relocating back here I don't want any Syndicate people moving in on any business I have in mind."

"Then don't worry about it, Mr. Bannerman. Unfortunately, in any state that has legalized gambling, there is a certain amount of outside interference and an influx of off-color characters. In this case, Matteau is clean and has applied for a gambling license although his location is not specified. Knowing local politics, I'd say he'll have it accepted. Nevertheless, he'll be well investigated and will comply with all state and local laws."

I eased out of the chair and said, "Thanks, Lieutenant. It's nice to know we're all safe from the criminal element."

For some reason he gave me a funny look, his eyes slitted almost shut and grinned right across his face. "It's nice to be appreciated, Mr. Bastard Bannerman."

I laughed at him, threw a wave and went back to my car. Fifteen minutes later I parked in the rear of the Bannerman Building on Main Street and took the elevator up to Rudy's office where the receptionist told me she was sorry, but nobody could see Mr. Bannerman without an appointment.

When I said I was Cat Bannerman and she had no choice she reached for the intercom until I switched it off and she took one look at my face and thought it better to head for the ladies' room.

My chubby cousin had a nice setup. All the accoutrements for the idle rich. A mahogany desk, antique furniture, a well organized bar, golf clubs stacked in the corner with parlor-putting devices in a rack on the wall, a couch under a row of book shelves, a stereo hi-fi set and TV built into the walls and that was the order of business.

Except for Rudy Bannerman. He was stretched out on the couch with a wet towel across his forehead and when he saw me he pulled the towel off and sat up with an expression of pure fear on his face.

"Hello, Cousin," I said. I toed a chair in close to the couch and sat down. "You're shook, cousin. You're thinking of what it feels to be a killer. You're going through the pain of relief because they finally caught up with Guy Sanders."

"Cat . . ." He licked his lips nervously.

"I'll tell you, cousin, but first I want some answers. Talk back or hand me any crap and I'll slap you silly. We're not kids any more. You're not a few years older and twenty pounds heavier where it counts. Now you're older and a pig and I can tear your ears off."

He couldn't take it. He flopped back on the couch reaching for the towel. I said, "You had a picture of Irish Maloney in your room. Where did you get it?"

"I . . . from the display at the Club."

"Why?"

He came up from the couch, his face livid. "I don't have to put up with this! I'm going to call the police. I'm . . ."

"Knock it off."

Rudy looked like he was going to have some kind of attack. He came apart in little pieces until his round body began to heave with jerky sobs and once again he went back into the contour of the couch and stayed there.

"I asked you a question. If you want the police, they can ask it."

"She . . . was nice."

"How often did you see her?"

"She didn't want to see me. I was a Bannerman and that tramp . . ."

"How often, Rudy?"

"A . . . few times, that's all. She . . . she didn't like me."

"I wonder why."

"She didn't have to say the things she did."

"How did you kill him, Rudy?"

His head rolled toward the wall. "I don't remember. I was . . . drunk. Sick."

"When did they put the bite on you?"

"Who?"

"Gage and Matteau. When did they make their offer?" I asked him.

"Two days later. They . . . went to father. He had Vance see them. There was nothing we could do. Nothing at all." His voice trailed off to a whisper."

"When do they want the dough, Rudy?"

He was on his side now, not able to look at me at all. He was like a baby in bed, seeking the comfort of crib and covers. "Saturday," he got out.

Three days from now. To get a million bucks up meant a lot of converting and it wasn't going to be easy and here was this slob sitting on his tail crying. Whatever stocks and properties were going into the pot for this little venture must be damn negotiable to be taken so lightly. In this day of taxes and paperwork a million bucks to line a hood's pockets wasn't easy to lay hold of. Taxes alone on that kind of loot would be enormous.

"Who's handling the arrangements, Rudy?"

"Vance . . . he's doing everything."

"Why him?"

"Father is . . . sick. He gave Vance our power of attorney."

I climbed out of the chair and started towards the door. This time Rudy turned over when he heard me leaving. The pathos on his face was disgusting. "What're you . . . going to do, Cat?"

"I don't know," I said. "Maybe I'll turn you in and watch you burn."

Petey Salvo lived in the house he had been born in. There was a kid in a carriage, a couple more under school age tearing the flower beds up and a twelve year old boy sick in bed with a cold. The others were in their classrooms and Petey was trying to grab a bite and argue with his wife at the same time.

At least I got him off the hook in a hurry. A Bannerman coming to visit the Salvos was the biggest day in her life and when he introduced me the busty doll in the pink housecoat with a headful of curlers almost broke a track record getting into the bedroom to get herself straightened out and when she came back she looked at her husband with a totally different look in her eyes and I knew from then on things were going to be different around there. Petey caught the bit too and winked at me over his coffee cup and told her to blow with a voice of authority and like a dutiful wife she left bowing and scraping like I was the baron of Bannerman Estates. Luckily, he didn't mention I was the bastard one.

He shoved some biscuits my way and I buttered up. "How're your contacts around town, Petey?"

"Like what?"

"Two hoods are in from Chi. I want them located." I gave him their names and descriptions and he took them down in his head.

"No trouble. Maybe need a day."

"Too long."

"So I put out the word and we grab 'em. These the same ones hit you in the motel?"

"That's right."

"I thought so. I was wondering when you was gonna move in. You never let yourself get took before."

"I had a reason, Petey."

"Figured that too. How do you want to work it?"

"Just get 'em spotted. I'll do the rest."

"Like hell, Cat. If this ties in with Chuck I want part of it."

"You'll get cut in, buddy. I have a feeling I'm going to need you."

"You'll buzz me in a coupla hours. I'll see what I can do, okay?"

"Got it."

Simon Helm had had visions of money dangled before his eyes. He was waiting for me with photostats of the records he had accumulated and all the additional information he had picked up. He pulled a chair out for me, got behind the desk and swung the folder around for me to view his massive efforts in my behalf. "There it is, Mr. Bannerman, but I'm afraid it's all too late. Vance Colby picked up the option on that property for ninety thousand dollars. The option to be exercised within three months. The property alone is worth in the vicinity of a quarter million and his proposed installation will go a half million, at least. At this point I don't know if he is acting for himself, or another party, but in view of his past and knowing his method of operation, I'd say he was simply first man in a deal. You understand?"

"I get the picture. The property is out, right?"

"Definitely. The money has changed hands. The option has been signed. I'm afraid you'll have to consider other properties."

I shoved my hat back and wiped my face. "Guess I'll have to. I'll take a run out and look at the other places tomorrow. Sorry to put you to all the trouble."

"No trouble at all, Mr. Bannerman. Take your time and if you need any help, just call on me."

"Thanks, Mr. Helm, I will. Count on it."

I got gas down the corner and put in a call to the house. Annie answered and when I asked for Anita, put her on. I said, "Cat, honey."

"Where are you?"

"In town. You have any news?"

When she spoke her voice was hushed. "Uncle Miles is in his room with Teddy. They've had people here all day and didn't want me around. That one man was here too."

"The older guy, Matteau?"

"That's the one." Very softly she said, "Cat . . . what's happening?"

"Trouble, baby. Where's Vance?"

"He just left. It was . . . terrible. They won't back down. They want all that money and . . ."

"Don't worry about it, Anita."

"I heard that . . . that . . . Matteau tell Vance . . . if he didn't get everybody straightened out somebody else would get killed. He's vicious. Cat . . . please help us, please. Vance is doing all he can, converting all his properties to help Uncle Miles. Cat, I'm frightened."

"Relax, doll. I'm beginning to get ideas. You just sit tight, hear?"

"I can't. Oh, please, Cat, do something."

"I will, baby," I said. "I will."

I hung up and stared at the phone a moment. A lot had fallen into place, now it was time to play the calculated hunches. I made a collect call to the coast and got Marty Sinclair and gave him the dope I wanted. I told him to push it and reach me anytime at night at the motel if he had to, otherwise I'd call him back tomorrow.

Then I went home. I parked the car, opened the door, walked in and flipped on the light. She was laying there naked as a jaybird on my bed with her clothes strewn all over the floor and a cigarette burning in her fingers.

I said, "How'd you get in here, Irish?"

"Told the desk clerk I was your wife." She held up her hand with the rings on it. "He simply looked at this and thought you'd appreciate the surprise. Do you?"

"Love it. You don't mourn long, do you?"

"Hardly a minute, Mr. Bannerman."

I looked at her sharply and she caught it.

"Cat Cay Bannerman," she said. "The desk clerk told me that too. Like you said, you *are* big. But you didn't know Chuck in the Marines, did you?"

"No."

"Then you must have come to see me."

"Right."

"Why?"

"I was checking out a motive for your husband's murder. A good nympho can get a lot of guys killed. I wanted to see how well you knew Rudy Bannerman."

"And I told you."

I put it to her bluntly. "There was somebody else . . . not Sanders. You were seen with him several times."

"Mr. Bannerman, there have been many others."

"This one was there often. Late."

Irish Maloney wouldn't have made a dime playing poker. She frowned, thought a moment and said, "There was Arthur Sears. I liked him."

"What was he like?"

"Good looking, money, big fancy Buick, treated a woman real nice. He was in love with me." She grinned and squirmed on the bed. "He wanted me to leave Chuck and go away with him. He said he'd do anything for me and he meant it too. I like that, men wanting to do all those things for me."

"Why didn't you go?"

"And have Chuck slap me silly? Besides, he didn't have *that* kind of money. When I go, I want to go first class. That takes the big kind. He knew what I meant."

I walked over and sat down, stretching out my legs. Irish tensed herself and spread out all across the bed, her eyes languid, watching every move I made. "Why aren't you working tonight?" I asked her.

"Because I was waiting for you. Petey told me where you stayed. I told you I was coming to get you."

"Maybe I'll toss you out on your can."

"You won't."

"Why not?"

"You want me too, that's why." She reached her arms out. "Come, man."

I didn't want to, but it had been too long. I made all the mental excuses, then I got up and went over to her. She was big and voluptuous and ready and I was there. And ready too. And I found out why any man could get a crazy desire for someone like her, even if he was Rudy Bannerman.

CHAPTER SEVEN

I got up before she was awake, showered and left a note for her to get home and I'd see her later, then I went out and phoned Petey Salvo. It hadn't taken the big guy long to pinpoint Gage and Matteau. They were both staying at the Orange House on Main Street and had spent the night before making the rounds of the clubs winding up at the Cherokee doing nothing more than having a few drinks and watching the action at the tables. About two o'clock Gage had gotten pretty jumpy and Matteau had taken him out. Petey had the idea Gage was a hophead and had to go somewhere to mainline one and he didn't know how right he was. He was all for going down and nailing the pair in their hotel but I vetoed it and told him to hang on until I pulled the cork myself.

At the restaurant I picked up the latest piece of news. Guy Sanders was on his way back to Culver City and the trial date had been set. Time was running out on the sucker.

Hank Feathers was still in bed when I got there. Waking him up wasn't easy and he came out of the pad swearing up a storm. I even made the coffee and it wasn't until he had two of them down that he began to act normal. He was sore because he had to spend a couple of hours with Lieutenant Travers going over my history and couldn't find one thing to say except that he knew my old man, I was a Bannerman and that was it. I wasn't about to fill him in all the way and he knew it.

He said, "You sure raised hell downtown, son."

"It's about time somebody did."

"Fine, fine, but they dragged me in. When a Bannerman yells around here everybody jumps. You put the needle into Travers about those two guys and he's got the lines burning all over the state. You know the pitch?"

"Suppose you tell me."

"For six years the Syndicate has been trying to move in here. They got a few places started but the state pushed them out. So now they got a toehold again. Matteau's filed as a resident and even though they know he's tied up with a bunch in Chicago they can't prove it or do a damn thing about it. He's got power behind him and it moves all the way to the Capitol. Brother, this town's got trouble."

"So stick around and get a good story. You still ready to step on toes?"

"Bannermans'?"

"Anybody's."

"I'm a reporter, son. Somebody steps out of line, it's news and I get it printed. What have you got going?"

"Throw a monkey wrench into the Sanders thing.

Make it look like a trial of political expediency. Hit the D.A. and get the paper to press for a full investigation . . . anything to delay the trial. Give it enough coverage so they won't be able to get a jury that hasn't read or heard about it. Can you do that?"

"Sure, but I may get canned and I'm almost at retirement age."

"Take a chance."

"Boy, do I live dangerously."

"Don't we all," I said.

Petey Salvo got me into the *Cherokee Club* before anyone was there and I headed for the kitchen. He dug around in the cutlery drawers a few minutes pulling out every form of knife they had there until he had a sample spread out on the butcher's block of every one. Most were of the common variety, there was one I picked up and scrutinized carefully before I put it in my inside pocket wrapped in a napkin.

"What're you gonna do with that?" Petey asked me.

"Give it to the police surgeon who examined Chuck's wound."

"The guy said he got it with a stiletto."

"Look at the steak knives, friend. They're specialty numbers and might do it. Instead of tossing the murder weapon away, suppose a killer simply put it back in service. A check shows nothing gone, a weapon was available, and what happens?"

"You got me," he said. "What?"

"A killer gets away with murder."

Because I was a Bannerman, Dr. Anthony Wember was willing to make the comparison. He was sceptical, but had to admit there was a possibility that the knife I offered might have inflicted the wound. He couldn't be certain because of the peculiar nature of the cutting and puncturing combination in Maloney's chest, but it was a thought and he would consider it. He had gone to great lengths to establish the nature of the weapon and a stiletto type it was; pointed, sharp along one length at least, straight blade with a rising center. He seemed to think both edges had been ground, but again, it was speculation. The doctor said he'd check it again to be sure and would make the information available.

At least to a Bannerman.

When we left it was time to do the other thing. Petey was all smiles when we got to the Orange House because he knew the ropes and how to work it and got a pimply faced kid in a bellboy's uniform to get the key we wanted. I knocked while he stayed out of the way and when Popeye Gage opened the door he wasn't a bit worried because he had a gun in his fist and said, "Hey Carl, look who we got. The punk's back and asking for it."

Matteau looked up from his paper, put it down and stood up with a grin wreathing his face. "Couldn't take a lesson, could you, boy?"

"I told you not to call me that." I started toward him fast.

"Hold it," Gage said. He walked up behind me and let me feel the muzzle of the rod. I maneuvered them just right so I had them with their backs to the door and they didn't hear Petey come in and never knew he was in the room until he slammed their heads together with an unearthly crack that put them unconscious on the floor for an hour.

But it took us that long to shake the place down. We came up with three .38's, a half a case of booze and forty-two hundred bucks in cash, but that was all.

Popeye Gage was the first one to open his eyes. He saw Petey leaning over him and tried to fake it, but the act didn't hold. Petey dragged him to his feet and held him up against his chest and you never saw fear in a guy's eyes before unless you saw his.

I said, "Put him in the chair, Petey. We have something special for him."

"Let me give him something special, Cat."

"Save it for the other one. I know what will make this one talk."

Petey threw Popeye halfway across the room into an overstuffed chair and the punk cringed there shivering because he found something that didn't play out the way he thought it would and he was almost ready to hurt.

Carl Matteau wasn't quite so easy. He had gone the

route before too and decided to take it cursing and swearing all the way, but no matter what Petey did to him he wasn't about to spill his guts. I was figuring on that and let him go through the rough stuff until the blood ran down his chin and his eyes were rolling in their sockets and said, "We want the knife, Carl. What do we do to get it?"

"Go screw yourself."

I hit him myself this time. I laid one on him that sent him out of the seat to the wall and he sat there on the floor glowering at me.

"You hit the wrong one, buddy. You're in a trap now."

He said two words.

Petey gave him one then and he went out cold.

Over in the corner Popeye Gage started to whimper. Petey said, "They done it, right?"

"They didn't done it," I told him. "They were just part of it."

"I'll kill 'em if you want, Cat. We can dump ..."

"No killing, Petey. Don't involve yourself."

"Chuck was my friend."

"So we'll stick them. Only don't let's take a fall, oke?"

"You're calling it, Cat."

I went over to Gage and stood there looking at him for a minute. I said to Petey, "You know a place where we can put this one? Some place where he can't be heard and nobody can hear him scream?"

"There's the smokehouse behind your place, remember?"

Remember? Damn right I remembered. I had taken enough beatings from Miles there often enough when Rudy and Teddy had made me take lumps.

"That should do it."

Popeye knew what I was getting at. He could see a couple of days going by without pumping a few shots of the big H into his veins and knew what would happen. His mouth worked until the words came out. "Look, I don't know nothing. I don't . . ."

"It's only what the others don't know, little man. That's what counts. They'll all think Carl clued you in, so sweat. Sweat hard," I said.

We left Carl Matteau like that and drove six miles

back to the Bannerman place and locked Popeye in the smokehouse. He went quietly because Petey laid a short one on his jaw and left him on a pile of sawdust. When he woke up he'd be screaming for a shot and would be ready to say anything if we'd get him a fix.

I had Petey wait in the car and took the back door route to the house again. Annie had a ready smile, her hands and clothes white with flour. She told me Rudy had come home sick yesterday and was still in bed. Cousin Teddy left town on some mission and Uncle Miles was in the library with Vance Colby.

Rather than push on in, I stood there, listening to the heated voice coming from inside. The oak doors were too thick to transmit the words but it was Vance Colby that was doing the demanding and Uncle Miles aquiescing little by little. When their discussion came to an end I pulled back, let Vance Colby through without him seeing me, and after he was out and in his car I went inside to where Miles was hunched up behind his desk, his face looking like he had just been whipped.

"Hello, Uncle."

"I don't think you and I have anything to discuss."

"No?"

It wasn't *what* I said. It was the way I said it. His mouth started to hang open and I saw his hands shake. "What . . . do you mean?"

We *did* have something to discuss, all right, but I didn't know what it was. As long as he thought I did he was on the hook, not me. "I got the picture pretty well laid out," I told him, a grin on my face.

Miles looked like he was going to die right there. He'd make a lousy poker player too. He'd said enough with his face to show me not to push any further so I let out a chuckle and walked out of the room.

Anita was just coming down the stairs, saw me and hurried, both hands reaching for mine. Her voice was soft as she said, *"Cat, Cat caught the rat."* When we were kids and she said that I used to chase her until I caught her and held her down squealing and kicking making like I was going to feed her a worm. It had been a great game.

"Hi, beautiful. Busy today?"

"Well, Vance . . ."

"He just left."

A frown creased her forehead. "That's funny. He didn't call me."

"Big business."

I walked toward the kitchen with her, my arm circling her waist. She fitted up against me unconsciously, her thigh rubbing mine. "He's been like that for a month now. He's . . . changed."

"Feel like doing a little touring with me?"

"Where, Cat?"

"Just around. I have some stops to make."

"Okay," she smiled happily, "let me get my jacket."

On the way to town I checked in the office of the motel to see if I had any calls. There were two, one from Sam Reed in Chicago and the other from Hank Feathers. I put the one through to Chicago first and got Sam at his place just as he was about to leave.

"Cat," he said, "I got a little more on Matteau. Guy I know pretty well used to work with him and when I got around to asking about him he let loose some odds and ends."

"Let's have them."

"The Syndicate didn't just move in down there. They were approached by somebody with a deal. They never would have touched the area after all the trouble they had the last time, but this deal looked solid and they went for it. Seems legit and Matteau is going to head it up. If it swings the Syndicate will get in good, but it's got to be legit. They can handle things once they're established. Now, that do you any good?"

"It makes sense, Sam. Thanks for calling."

"No trouble. Like I said, I'll be wanting a favor some day."

"You'll get it."

I held down the cutoff bar, let it up and gave the operator the out of town number for Hank Feathers. He was in a hotel a hundred miles away on an assignment they threw at him the last minute and had tried to locate me earlier and couldn't. I said, "What's up, doc?"

"Something you'll have to run down personally. The printer at the paper . . . the one who lives near Irish Maloney . . . well, his wife forgot to tell me something. One of her constant visitors backed into a parked car one night and never left a calling card. Minor damage, but she just happened to be coming home, saw the accident and took his license number and stuck it under the windshield wiper of the car he bumped."

"A neighborhood car?"

"Can't say. She didn't keep a record. She was just indignant about him running off."

"When did it happen?"

"A couple of weeks ago."

"Good deal. I'll see what I can do."

"One more thing . . . will you get over and see old man Wilkenson? He's bugging me on the hour. Get him off my back. So he'll yak for a couple hours about the old days, but then it's over."

"Yeah, sure. See you when you get back."

"Two, three days. No more."

Anita looked at me curiously when I got back in the car. "Are we going someplace?"

I nodded. "Making house calls. You're going to see an insurance investigator at work. At least I hope everybody thinks so."

"Why?"

"Because all this trouble the Bannermans are in has an answer and it's not the one you think it is."

"I thought you didn't care about them."

"I don't baby, not one damn bit. Only you. If it touches you then I'm involved too. As long as you're wearing the Bannerman name it's going to stay clean one way or another. I told you . . . there's not one thing I want from them. I was out a long time ago. I'm the bastard Bannerman, I never had anything and never wanted anything. In a way I'm lucky. What I never had I don't miss. I can work things out for myself and although I don't eat high off the hog I manage to keep my stomach full. I'm free and clear because I don't own enough to get into debt over. Don't think there weren't times when I envied Rudy and Teddy all they had. I used to hate their guts because they had it all and took what little I had away too. But it's over now and that's it. For you I'm pushing, no other reason."

"I love you, Cat. I shouldn't say it, but I do. I always have."

"I know, kitten."

"Cat . . . there's nothing I can do. It's . . . it's too late."

"Is it?" My voice felt tight and funny. I let the clutch in and pulled away.

We took the area a block at a time and rang doorbells, going back to the empty places until we caught someone home. We didn't have a bit of luck tracing the car until six thirty when I had about four houses to go. A woman came by with an arm load of groceries, saw me getting into the car and stopped me. I had used a fake name all along and almost didn't hear her when she said, "Oh . . . Mr. Wells . . ."

Anita pointed past me. "She's calling you, Cat."

"Yes?" I remembered her from one of the first calls.

"I was mentioning your visit to my husband when he came home. Well, it wasn't our car, but a friend of his who was staying overnight. He found his car damaged in the morning with the man's license number on his windshield."

"That's just fine, ma'm. We'd like to settle the matter as soon as possible, so if you can give me his name I'll get right to him."

"Certainly." She shifted her packages. "Jack Jenner . . . and he lives on Third Avenue North. He's in the book."

"Thank you. This has been a great help."

At the first pay station I stopped, looked up Jenner in the phone book and dialed his number. He seemed surprised to hear from me because so far he hadn't done anything about the incident. He read the license number out to me, I told him to process it as quickly as he could, thanked him and hung up.

One crack in the wall. That's all you need. There's always a chink somewhere that is the weakest point and can bring the whole structure down in ruins.

Anita said, "Have you found it?"

"Almost. There's a shadow figure in the picture and

when the light hits we'll know for sure. Let's go back to my motel. I want to clean up and we can eat."

"I was supposed to see Vance. He'll . . ."

"He can wait. A kissin' cousin has some rights, hasn't he?"

"Uh-huh," she laughed, "but he'll be mad."

"What he needs is another poke in the mouth."

"He'll never forgive you for what you did to him."

"Tough. He was asking for it."

She nodded, not looking at me. "He's . . . always been like that. He had to fight his way up, you know . . . supported himself at school, started small in business and made everything the difficult way."

"What's new about that, kid? Someday I'll tell you my story."

I swung in at the motel and killed the engine. I opened the door, got one foot out when I saw the other car that was already nosed out start to move. The lights were off and if the top hadn't crossed the lights of the office I would have missed it. I yelled, "Down!" and gave Anita a shove that sent her on her back on the ground through the door on her side.

The blast of the gun came on top of the winking yellow light from the muzzle and a bullet smashed into the dashboard over my head sending glass fragments all over the place. I pulled the .45, thumbed the hammer back and let two go toward the car that was swerving in the gravel and heading back to town. From the angle I had to shoot I knew damn well that I had missed him, but they weren't sticking around for a shoot out. There could always be a second time.

I got Anita to her feet and inside as people came pouring out of their rooms. The clerk was shaking like a leaf, knocking on my door trying to find out what happened. I told him everything was all right . . . it was an attempted stickup that didn't come off and nobody got hurt.

But I was wrong. He had called the police the minute he heard the shots and Lieutenant Travers himself answered the call. He came in with a uniformed sergeant, closed the door and stood there with his hands behind his back. "Mr. Bannerman . . . I assume you have a reasonable explanation for the shooting."

I told him the stickup story and he didn't go for it.

His smile was pretty grim. "You know," he said, "I've had about enough of the Bannerman crap. They think they can get away with anything in this town and most of the times they can. I've been read off too often by my superiors who were under pressure and took too much lip from cheap politicians too many times. I think this time I'll nail me a Bannerman." His smile got colder with each word. "We had a complaint that you carry a gun. This so?"

There was no sense denying it. I nodded toward the chair where it lay under my coat.

Travers said, "Get it, Fred."

I knew what was coming next and started to get dressed. When I finished he said, "Let's go. All the talking you can do at headquarters with witnesses and someone to take your statement." He looked at Anita. "You too, miss."

CHAPTER EIGHT

They sat us down around a table, my gun laying there in the middle and Travers looking pleased with himself. He had given Anita the opportunity to make a phone call and she got Vance Colby. He was on the way over.

In the meantime I made small talk, got the point across that I'd like some representation myself and after Travers thought it over he told the sergeant to plug in the phone. I got Wilkenson's name out of the book, told him who I was and where I was and asked him to get over fast. He was too excited to talk, but said he'd be there as quickly as possible.

For a ninety-three year old man he did a good job. He

made it in five minutes. I hadn't seen him in twenty-five years and it looked as if he hadn't aged a bit. He was tall, topped with a bushy white head of hair, a manner that was positive and honest and it was easy to see why George P. Wilkenson was the most respected counsellor in the state.

We shook hands and his grip was firm. I was ready for a lot of gab, then got fooled there too. He asked Travers if he could speak to me alone for a few minutes and Travers was glad to grant him the courtesy. From his expression I knew what he was thinking . . . it would take a lot of talking to get me off the hook and it wasn't about to happen.

The tiny room we sat in stunk of stale sweat and cigar smoke and the edge of the table was notched with cigarette burns. I had seen too many of these rooms to enjoy being in one again. Wilkenson threw his briefcase on the table, pulled out a sheaf of papers and thrust them toward me, fanning them out so I could see the signature lines he had marked off.

"Cat," he said, "your father trusted me, so did your grandfather. Do you?"

"Why not?"

"Very well then." He held out a pen. "Sign where indicated."

I wrote my name in about twenty places, handed the pen back and stacked the papers together. "What was that all about?"

"Did you ever know the details of your grandfather's will?"

I made a noncommittal gesture with my hands. "He split it with my old man and Miles, didn't he?"

"Up to a point, yes. There were certain other provisions. After their death the unspent capital would go to their children. If the children die, the remainder would go to the other brother or his children."

"So?"

"The final provision was this. Your grandfather knew your father's habits. It was his idea that his children might inherit his casual attitude of neglect and fail to claim the money. In that event, if the capital belonging to the deceased brother was not claimed by his children within thirty years, the others took possession. That time period is up . . . this Saturday. Tomorrow."

I still didn't get it. "Okay, so I inherit a hundred percent of nothing. Why all the business. The old man blew his load in a hurry. I hope he had fun."

"Ah, that's the point, son. He didn't. He was footloose enough, but his material possessions were very few. The fun he had didn't cost much at all. When he died he left quite a few million dollars intact. After taxes you stand to inherit at least two of them."

I felt my fingers bite the edge of the table and without realizing it I was on my feet. *"What?"*

Wilkenson nodded slowly. "That's why the urgency of having you sign the claim."

Now the picture was laid out from all angles. I asked the next question. "Where do Miles and his kids come in."

"Nowhere, I'm afraid. They have gone through every cent they ever had. You are the only wealthy Bannerman left."

"Damn!"

"But there's one clause that may disrupt everything, son. It has me worried. You stand to face a very serious charge."

"What about it?"

"Your grandfather was a peculiarly virtuous old man. He was honest and law abiding to the extreme. He specified in the will that if any of the inheritors should ever be held and booked by the police on a criminal charge, and found guilty, they were to be cut off immediately and the money transferred to the others."

No wonder the Bannermans were so fussy about keeping out of trouble. Buy anything or anybody, as long as the cost was less than the eventual one.

"Lieutenant Travers intends to book you. Carrying concealed weapons is a criminal charge."

"You let me take care of that," I said.

He shook his massive head. "I'm afraid he can't be bought."

"You let me take care of that," I repeated.

Wilkenson studied me a moment regretfully. He had done his duty, fulfilled his commitment, and now there was nothing more to do except make out more papers. I grinned at him, tight and nasty. "Don't count me out. Not yet. First do me a favor."

"If I can."

"Get hold of Petey Salvo." I gave him a list of places where he could be located. "Tell him to get Carl Matteau and keep him with Gage until . . ." I looked at my watch, ". . . eleven o'clock tonight, then bring them to the Bannerman place. We'll be waiting."

He frowned at me. "But . . ."

"Just do it, okay?"

"Very well."

"Good. Now beat it. Don't let any of the others see you."

The sergeant took me back to the other room and there the clan was gathered; Miles, Rudy, Teddy and Vance. Anita had pulled away from him and looked at me anxiously when I came in and I didn't let my expression change at all. Except for Anita, they didn't seem a bit unhappy at all.

Vance said to Travers, "Now, sir, if it's all right with you, I would like to take Miss Bannerman home. It's been very trying for her."

The cop nodded agreement. "I know where to find her."

"Will there be any charges?"

"Oh, I don't think so," he said pleasantly. "She'll be a witness, naturally but as an innocent bystander. The one I want is right here." He pointed a long finger at me. I sat down and didn't look at them, but I managed a wink of confidence at Anita. She forced a smile, but her eyes were wet.

"Go on home, honey," I said. "It's not all that bad."

When they had gone Travers sat back, satisfied with himself, and said, "Now let's get to your statement."

I reached in my pocket and pulled out the license number I had gotten from the Jenner guy. "In the interests of harmonious relationships . . . and justice, how about finding out who owns the car that goes with this plate number."

He picked the slip from my fingers. "What kind of a game is this?"

"Do it, then I'll tell you. You might get a promotion out of it."

Travers was a guy who enjoyed games. Besides, he couldn't understand my attitude. It had something to do with the way he smiled at me the last time.

He called the sergeant in, told him to run it through, then sat there saying nothing, idly tapping a pencil on the desk. I played the game with him for fifteen minutes until the sergeant came back with a card, handed it to Travers who looked at it, not getting what it meant, then handed it to me.

I said, "Touché. You get your promotion."

Then we had a little talk.

When it was over I picked up my gun, put it on and told Travers to follow me back to the Bannerman place with his sergeant and went out to the Ford.

Ten forty-five. The lights were on downstairs in the library and when I went in I could hear their voices. No longer were they tense . . . there was an air of relief and jocularity there now. Only Anita didn't have a drink in her hand and Vance Colby was standing in front of the desk like the old master himself, overshadowing Miles who held down his usual position. Rudy and Teddy were toasting each other and both were half stiff already.

They sobered up pretty fast when I came in. Their faces got a flat, sour look and Miles suddenly looked pale. Only Vance regained his composure. "We hardly expected to see you here."

"I guess you didn't." I walked over to Anita and sat on the arm of her chair. Her hand reached for mine, squeezed it and she bit her lip to keep from crying.

Then I played the time game on them, just sitting there silently. At eleven on the dot Petey Salvo came through the door holding Gage and Matteau by their necks. Matteau had taken a beating somewhere along the line and Popeye Gage was in the first stages of narcotics withdrawal. All he wanted was a fix and would do anything to get it while he had the chance. Later, when the cramps hit him, he wouldn't be able to.

"Pretty," I said. "Nice company the Bannermans keep."

Rudy had to sit down. I wouldn't let him. "On your

feet, slob," I told him. "I want you to hear this standing up. I'm going to make you happy and sad all at once and I want to see what happens when I do."

"See here . . ." Vance started to say.

I waved a finger at him. "Not you, boy. You stay very, very quiet while I tell a story."

I said, "It started because this was a wide open state with legalized gambling and plenty of money to be made without too much work if the right deal could be swung. One man saw how he could do it. Cousin Rudy here made a sucker play for a ripe nympho named Irish Maloney and even if he didn't make out he established a motive for what was to come. The guy who spotted the move came into the family through a back door, knew what he was going to set up and made a contact with the Chicago Syndicate to borrow enough money to get his project rolling.

"The next step was easy. At the right time, when Rudy was drunk and sick, he got him to a toilet where he passed out, went outside and killed Chuck Maloney with a steak knife from the club, put the knife back, then had the Syndicate men put the word through that they had seen Rudy make the hit and that they had the evidence. *But all this while there was no evidence.*

"Then came the hitch . . . the money demand was going to fall through and how that must have shook up our killer. The Bannermans didn't have any loot left! Ah . . . but in a way, there was. Very shortly they were going to inherit my share of the wealth if I didn't claim it and there was little chance I would, so the killer was safe. A few more days and he'd have it made.

"Imagine how he felt when I showed up? Brother, he liked to 've browned out. The point was . . . he had spent the Syndicate money on initial expenses and unless he got his hands on the Bannerman money he couldn't carry it through and he knew damn well the Syndicate wouldn't stand for the loss without getting something in return. Like his life.

"So our boy tried to have me roughed up and scared out by Gage and Matteau. They didn't want me dead . . . just out of town long enough for the thirty year time period to expire. It didn't work. Now he got panicky. He even went as far as taking a shot at me himself. When that didn't work there was one other gimmick he had ready. He knew the details of the will and sent in a complaint that I carried a gun, a formidable charge if he could make it stick and one that would put my dough back in the hands of the other Bannermans. And three of them went for it. You know, I'm beginning to wonder just who the real bastard Bannermans are around here.

"Now our killer is really in a sweat because he doesn't know where I stand or what the next play is. He knows I have it locked but doesn't know how and has to hear me out to figure his next move.

"Funny how I found out about it. Real careless of him. He got the original idea because he liked the same dame Rudy liked and when he saw her under the phoney name of Arthur Sears she bragged about her men and up came the name of Rudy Bannerman . . . and an ex con called Sanders. When they interrogate Sanders he'll tell them an anonymous call told him about Chuck's murder and that he's to be the first grabbed and the guy panicked. I bet that night he had even gotten drunk with some unknown guy and was carried home where he couldn't prove an alibi. But . . . that will come out later.

"Anyway, our Arthur Sears made a bad move. He backed into a car and drove off. An indignant dame saw it and grabbed his number. Only the number didn't belong to any Arthur Sears. The name that went with it was Vance Colby."

The glass dropped from his hands and he took an uncertain step back against the desk and stood there clutching it. Anita had me so tightly I couldn't move my arm, but it was my left one and didn't matter I could still draw and fire with my right.

"The dirty part was that you didn't give a damn about Anita, Vance. She wasn't your type. When your history gets checked out we'll find that out. All you wanted was the Bannerman money and when you had it you would have dumped her fast. Nice, dirty thinking."

From the doorway Carl Matteau was watching Colby with a face that was a hard mask. I said, "You have several choices, Vance. You probably have that gun on you that you shot at me with today. Move toward it and I'll kill you right where you stand. I'll put a .45 between your horns that will rip off the back of your head and spatter the old man there with more brains and blood than he already has.

"The second choice, Colby. You go out the back way and run for it. You'll have the cops on your back all the way, but it won't be them you'll be worrying about. It'll be the Syndicate boys because when Matteau here passes the word along a contract goes out on you and it will be worse than anything the cops can do to you.

"Third choice, killer. Outside the front door is a police car. You can get in, go downtown with Lieutenant Travers and hope the courts will give you life rather than the chair.

"Fourth choice is to brazen it out and if you look at Petey Salvo's face you'll see what can happen. Chuck Maloney was his friend and Petey will go all the way for his buddies, dead or alive."

Vance Colby was dead white. There was no arrogance left in him now at all. He was a terrified animal with death facing him on all sides and all he could do was take the least of the evils. Very slowly he turned, looked at the open doors of the library to the hall beyond and started walking. He had company. Travers was back there and had heard it all. They went outside together and I heard the car start up and saw the red light on the top start to wink before they cleared the driveway.

I stood up and took Anita's hand. At the moment it was past her ability to comprehend, but soon she would see it. All she knew was that somehow she suddenly belonged to me and me to her and the world was ours at last. The two little Bannermans who never meant anything because the others loomed too large and too powerful.

They weren't that way now. I said, "You're broke, cousins. You'll have to sweat for it now. You can have the house and the property but it'll make you even broker so you'll have to think fast. Personally, I don't think you'll survive long and you can blame it on yourselves. I want nothing you ever had and I'm taking what was mine and you tried to steal. You have to live with yourselves and it won't be easy, and while you do you can be think-

ing that the Bastard Bannerman wasn't the real bastard
. . . it was you, the others. You're all bastards. I'm taking Anita out of here and I'll provide for Annie. I don't
think she wants any part of you any more."

I pulled Anita toward the door and turned around.
Rudy and Teddy had to sit down. It was too much for
them. "Adios, Cousins and Uncle." I said. "Work hard
and earn lots of money."

The night was clean, the sky peppered with stars and
the road a moonlit ribbon heading east. She sat next to
me as close as she could get and the radio played softly
while I tooled along at an even sixty. Since we got married back there she had hardly spoken and I kept waiting
for her to ask me.

She finally did. Curiosity, a trait of the Bannermans
who bore the Cat label.

"That Lieutenant Travers . . . he let you go. What
happened?"

"Nothing. I just told him who I was and where I was
going. He checked on it."

"Are we going there now?"

"Uh-huh."

"Can you tell me?"

I looked at her and laughed. "It may interfere with our
honeymoon, but it might be exciting at that. I'm picking
up an escaped prisoner in New York and driving him
back to the coast."

Amazement was written all over her. "But I thought
you . . . you . . ."

"Police, doll. I was going east on a vacation and they
let me have the assignment to save expenses."

"Oh, Cat . . ."

"Now I'll be like that millionaire cop on the TV show.
Should be fun." I patted her leg and she snuggled up
against me, warm and soft. "We'll have the honeymoon
when we get back," I said.

More Mystery and Suspense Fiction from SIGNET

☐ **HAIL, HAIL, THE GANG'S ALL HERE! by Ed McBain.** In this 87th Precinct mystery all of Ed McBain's detectives come together for the first time and they're all kept hopping. Some of the stories are violent, some touching, some ironic, but all are marked by the masterful McBain touch . . . the "gang" has never been better.
(#T5063—75¢)

☐ **DEATH TO MY BELOVED by Richard Neely.** A psychotic killer lashes vengeance from San Francisco to New York, leaving a scarlet trail of murder, blackmail and sex— and a publisher's empire falls in an explosion of scandal.
(#T4774—75¢)

☐ **THE MEPHISTO WALTZ by Fred Mustard Stewart.** A masterpiece in suspense and quiet (the most deadly) horror. Only the strongest will resist its subtly diabolic power.
(#Q4643—95¢)

☐ **KISS THE BOYS AND MAKE THEM DIE by James Yardley.** A lovely lady agent and her tough ex-cop boss chase across the Middle East in this fast-paced suspense thriller of international intrigue. (#T4395—75¢)

☐ **THE CHAIRMAN by Jay Richard Kennedy.** A teacher turned agent is sent on a dangerous assignment to China to find a "destruction machine." (#Q4255—95¢)